HIGH

IT'S THE STUFF OF NIGHTMARES

DATE WITH DEATH

She was going to die. Now. Right now. Because the face of the only person who could save her from plunging down upon those cruel, jagged rocks directly beneath her was no longer quite human. Every shred of decency, kindness, of forgiveness, of compassion, was gone, replaced by the unmistakable look of a predator.

DIANE HOH

HORROR HIGH

DATE WITH DEATH

SCHOLASTIC

Scholastic Children's Books
An imprint of Scholastic Ltd
Euston House, 24 Eversholt Street
London, NW1 1DB, UK
Registered office: Westfield Road, Southam, Warwickshire, CV47 0RA
SCHOLASTIC and associated logos are trademarks and
or registered trademarks of Scholastic Inc.

First published in the US as *Prom Date* by Scholastic Inc, 1996
First published in the UK by Scholastic Ltd, 1997
This edition published in the UK by Scholastic Ltd, 2009

Text copyright © Diane Hoh, 1996

ISBN 978 1407 11151 3

British Library Cataloguing-in-Publication Data
A CIP catalogue record for this book is available
from the British Library

The right of Diane Hoh to be identified as the author of this work
has been asserted by her.

Printed in the UK by CPI Bookmarque, Croydon, CR0 4TD
Papers used by Scholastic Children's Books are made from wood grown in
sustainable forests.

1 3 5 7 9 10 8 6 4 2

www.scholastic.co.uk/zone

Prologue

Late one balmy spring night when they were twelve, they sat around the blazing campfire on the beach at the Point, their spindly, adolescent legs crossed, their arms linked in companionship, their faces filled with trust in each other and faith in the future, and talked about how they would always be there for each other.

"Remember the night we took the oath?" one said with a self-conscious laugh, afraid they would be annoyed at her reminder of the childish ceremony held two years earlier in this very same spot. "My mother asked me what happened to my finger, and I told her I cut it peeling an apple. She would have had a fit if she knew we'd all deliberately sliced our fingertips and then taken an oath of friendship. Probably would have grounded me for a month."

The girl sitting beside her nodded. "Mine, too. When she said something about the dried blood on my finger, I pretended to be surprised and looked at it like I'd never even noticed the cut. I said I didn't know what had happened. And she believed me."

"That's because you're so nice," the first girl said. "Everyone always expects you to tell the truth. You could probably get away with murder if you wanted to. Who would ever suspect you?"

The wind shifted, and the flames stretched higher, as if they were reaching for the nearby trees. "We've kept our oath," a third girl said firmly. "We've been there for each other, just like we promised, and that will never change. Even when we're old and grey, we'll still be friends, right?"

"Right!" The fourth and tallest girl raised a clenched fist in the air. "One for all and all for one, that's our motto! We stick together through thick and thin. And we always will. No matter what."

On that balmy spring night as they danced along the cool sand with the wind tugging at their hair, if someone strolling by had asked if they expected to remain that close forever, they would all, without exception, have responded with youthful enthusiasm, "Of course. Always and forever!"

They would have been wrong.

One

The small dress shop known as Quartet in the heart of downtown Glenview was a frenzy of activity. Although the shop had four owners (hence the name), only one of them ran the shop. Adrienne Dunne was a tall, attractive woman with intelligent grey eyes behind horn-rimmed glasses, her auburn hair tied back in a neat chignon at the nape of her neck. Dressed in a stunning pink suit, she calmly wove her way in and out of the throng of young women who were excitedly exclaiming over and trying on the prom dresses in the shop, most of which Adrienne had designed and made herself. She gave advice, found selections for girls overtaken by confusion, and measured for alterations when they were needed.

Her two helpers, her daughter Megan and Megan's best friend, Jade LaSalle, were not so calm. Neither anticipated such a hectic Saturday afternoon. They had expected the girls to come in one or two at a time, rather than in this unrestrained herd. Megan was reminded of a cattle stampede in an old Wild West film. Then, too, they were discovering what a knife in the heart it was to help other girls search for the perfect dress to wear to the senior prom. The prom Megan and Jade did not expect to attend.

It wasn't as if either girl was unattractive. Both were tall and thin, moved gracefully, and had good skin. Great skin. Megan had never had a blemish in her life. She was fair, with light brown, very fine, straight hair, which she wore shoulder-length and tended to yank away from her face and tie back. She had amazing eyes: doe-shaped, a warm, deep brown, with long, thick, upturned eyelashes. Intelligent and a born leader, Megan would have been, in a perfect world, form captain. Unfortunately, at Glenview High, intelligence, even when combined with a quick wit, wasn't enough. At Glenview, pretty and popular were also required if you were going to be elected for anything.

Both girls dated occasionally. But Megan had never dated one boy exclusively for any length of time. She hadn't yet met anyone she felt like saving all of her evenings for, and the feeling had been mutual because as far as she knew, she hadn't broken any hearts.

Because she loved to read, she really didn't mind spending time alone. Besides, she had Jade, who didn't date much, either, and Sophie and Lucy. They wouldn't be going to the prom, either. Maybe they'd all rent a dvd, and just have fun.

Many people who came into the shop mistook the two girls for sisters. But they really didn't look that much alike. While Jade, like Megan, was tall and slender, her face was thinner, with more sharp edges, her hair a cross between bronze and what Jade herself called "muddy water." "Like *burned* muddy water," she sometimes remarked sourly. Her eyes were a little green, a little grey. This was very disturbing to Jade, who would have preferred a clear, bright turquoise. She planned to buy turquoise contact lenses when she had enough money saved.

While Megan rejected every one of her mother's attempts to "beautify" her ("Megan, sweetie, you have such a pretty face. A little blusher, a touch of mascara, what harm can it do?"), Jade eagerly devoured every little self-improvement hint Adrienne dropped her way. Jade tried them all – sometimes it helped, sometimes it didn't. An experiment gone sour, something for the Other Girls, the ones who always somehow looked as if they belonged on the cover of a magazine, to laugh at. Not always behind Jade's back, either.

It was about to happen again. Leah Markham, tall and leopard-sleek, her dark hair spilling over her shoulders like black velvet, smiled with fake friendliness at Jade and asked with equally fake innocence, "Is that supposed to be a

5

chignon on the back of your head, Jade? Funny how it doesn't look anything like Adrienne's." She was holding a black velvet dress by its hanger.

Megan hated it that the "Pops" (her word for the popular girls) called her mother by her first name, but Adrienne said it was good for business.

The shop was packed with customers. Everyone in it heard Leah's cruel remark.

Jade turned scarlet and one hand flew to the back of her neck in embarrassment.

Megan, in the process of removing a pale pink dress from the rack, hissed over her shoulder, "Leah, let me just go and check in the back and see if we have a broom and a tall, pointed black hat to go with that dress."

Leah's friend, Beth Andrews, who always said hi to Megan at school, laughed. And tall, blonde Zoe, another of the Pops, scolded mildly, "Leah, don't be such a pain. Mind your manners."

Ignoring the reprimand, Leah said coldly, "You know, Megan, we don't *have* to buy our prom dresses here. We could go somewhere else and spend our money if you'd prefer."

Megan preferred. Megan wished for, *craved* their departure. Unfortunately, her mother didn't. Running your own business, from what Megan had seen, wasn't a great way to get rich. It was a constant struggle, like swimming upstream. She shouldn't be screwing it up for her mother, who worked harder than any other person Megan knew.

"You could go to every shop in town," Megan said to Leah, her voice smooth and controlled, "and not find anything that comes close to my mother's designs, and you know it. But if ordinary is what you want, there's the door. I'll even open it for you."

Because the girl knew Megan was right, she shrugged, fell silent, and resumed browsing through the lovely creations on the racks.

Jade went into the back room. When she returned to the sales floor, her sharp, angled face was grim, her attempt at a chignon gone. Her bronze hair hung loosely, limply, round her shoulders in her customary style.

Megan burned with anger. OK, maybe it hadn't been a perfect little bun, and maybe Jade was too young for such a sophisticated hairstyle. But she'd tried. It was mean of Leah to make fun of Jade for trying. One more example (and there were so many) of the Perfectly Pretty People stepping on the Imperfect. Mean. Really mean.

Joseph Noonan burst into the shop, all awkward arms and legs and freckles, a green baseball cap worn backwards over his bushy red hair. He was beaming with enthusiasm for his new part-time job. Adrienne had hired him to drive Quartet's van, making deliveries and picking up supplies.

Megan knew it wasn't just the job that lit up Joseph's round face. He was now in the presence of Jade LaSalle. Joseph had a thing for Jade, who so far seemed to regard him as a pesky younger brother or a mosquito tormenting her at a picnic. Joseph's blue eyes followed Jade's every movement adoringly. He sometimes brought her a single yellow rose when he came back from a delivery, and would have carried her books to the ends of the earth and back if Jade had asked him to. Jade was not impressed. If she thought of Joseph at all, it was only as a friend.

"One of these days," Megan had warned her, "he's going to get tired of being treated like the contents of a vacuum cleaner bag and find someone else. And you're going to miss him."

Megan liked Joseph. So he wasn't cool, like the gorgeous, athletic guys the Pops dated. So what? He was smart and funny and treated her mother with respect. Megan liked that about Joseph.

Jade was not so easily impressed.

Megan had said, "Jade, beggars can't be choosers. You're dying to go to the prom. I know Joseph's only a sophomore, but you're a senior, so you can invite anyone you want. Stop being such a snob. You're almost as bad as the Pops."

That, of course, was meant as an insult, and Jade took it that way. Still, she insisted stubbornly, "I'm not making do. I can do better than Joseph, I know I can. And if I can't, I'll just stay at home."

Megan gave up. Jade had her heart set on attending her senior prom with some tall, cool, popular guy. She refused to accept that they were all taken. David Goumas would be taking gorgeous Lily Pappas, who was one of the Pops but wasn't with them now because she never shopped at Quartet. Lily went into the city for her wardrobe. Jordan Nelson would be arm in arm with Beth, and Zoe would probably go with Dan McGill, unless she decided to ask a college guy. That was a concept Megan couldn't grasp. Asking someone else instead of going with Dan McGill? Crazy. He was so cute. Michael Danz, the poor fool, would be going with Leah Markham. Leah was a prime candidate for queen this year. Beth was a possibility, too, although she had a quieter kind of beauty, far less spectacular than Leah's. Lily and Zoe, who'd been dating seniors for years, had been queen already, and the rule at Glenview High was, only one monarchy to a customer.

Not that Leah wouldn't make a suitable queen. She certainly had a talent for ordering people around.

The point was, the best guys were already taken. If Jade wanted to attend the prom, she'd better lower her sights pretty fast or she'd be sitting at home watching rented dvds with her fellow wallflowers, Megan Dunne, Sophie Baker, and Lucy Dowd.

"Oh, come off it, Megan," Jade had said in exasperation the last time Megan had vented her opinion. "You could go, too. Lots of guys like you. I know a couple of juniors who think you're cute. They haven't asked you because they just don't think you're interested. If you want, I could drop some hints. Let them know you'd say yes if they asked."

"They won't ask," Megan said firmly. "I like them and they like me OK, I guess. But not as a date. They don't see me that way. I'm good old Megan, who can toss a ball or Frisbee with the best of them and help them with their maths, but that's about it. The image of me in a prom dress would be as hard for them to grasp as the meaning of a Shakespeare sonnet. So forget it, Jade. Just butt out, OK?"

"Look who's talking."

"Zoe," they heard Leah say authoritatively, "red is definitely not your colour. You're blonde. Find something more pastel, like this pale turquoise. It's perfect for you." She waved a dress in the air.

Megan knew exactly what she was doing. She wanted the red one for herself. Crafty Leah.

"It's no big deal, Leah," Zoe said, reaching for the turquoise. "If you really want the red one, here, take it. Just don't ever say I refused to give you the shirt off my back. Or dress, in this case."

From behind her, Megan heard Jade gasp in dismay. The turquoise! Jade had had her heart set on that dress ever since Adrienne finished hemming it and carefully slipped it onto a padded hanger. Maybe she wouldn't ever get to wear it. But it would crush her if someone else went to the prom in that dress.

Swiftly, Megan slid her right hand across the fat, wet sponge sitting in a small, white dish beside the cash register. The sponge was used to moisten stamps. Hurrying over to Leah's side, she grabbed the dress from her, saying, "Oh, sorry, that dress has a water stain on it," at the same time surreptitiously wiping her wet, gluey hand on the skirt. Then she pointed. "Look, see it, right there? It wasn't supposed to be on display. Off to the cleaners it goes!" she cried cheerfully, and swept the dress out of the room, ignoring Leah's indignant, "Well! I guess we should be checking the merchandise more carefully before we try it on. I didn't think that was necessary here."

"I didn't think that was necessary here!" Megan mimicked under her breath as she hung the turquoise dress in the wardrobe.

When Megan went back out on the floor, her other two best friends, Sophie and Lucy, had arrived. They were the only girls in the shop not shopping for prom dresses. They did not look happy.

11

And Leah was indeed wearing the red dress, a short, slinky number with spaghetti straps. Zoe was wearing black, and Beth looked lovely in a slender pale blue slip dress. All three dresses needed minor alterations. Adrienne promised to attend to them well ahead of the prom, still three weeks away.

When Leah brought her red dress to the counter to pay for it, Sophie and Lucy were lounging nearby, waiting for a chance to talk to Megan, "So," Leah asked them in a perfectly friendly voice, "did you two come to see what everyone's wearing to the prom? I guess this will be your only chance, since you won't be there."

Lucy, who was short and stocky, her bright blonde hair cut in a bob, flushed angrily and said, "You don't know that, Leah. Maybe *all* of us are going."

Leah laughed. "Right. Well, good, if you are, because then you'll get to see *me* crowned queen."

Sophie, as tall and thin as a stick, red hair frizzed round a narrow face, muttered, "I'd be happy to crown you myself, Leah, right here and now," but Leah had already turned back to Megan to hand her a piece of plastic.

As Megan slid the credit card through the machine, Leah smiled a smile as plastic as the card and said, "It must be hard selling all these beautiful dresses when you're not going to be wearing one yourself. Poor Megan." She glanced over at Jade, fastening "sold" tags on the dresses, and added, "I guess you won't be going, either, am I right, Jade?"

Jade winced and blanched. Megan Dunne, who had never physically hurt another human being in her entire life, found herself thinking how satisfying it would be to reach out with the scissors at her elbow and whack off every strand of Leah's silken dark locks, leaving her virtually bald. Instead, she said softly, "Leah, is that a spot I see right smack in the middle of your forehead?"

And even though there wasn't a blemish anywhere on that perfect porcelain skin, Megan felt a wickedly satisfying surge of triumph when Leah went as white as Jade had and her right hand flew up to explore her face in alarm. Even when her fingers felt nothing, she was compelled to sidestep over to the nearest mirror and peer in anxiously, just to be certain.

When she was satisfied, she said angrily, "That wasn't funny, Megan."

"Oh, yeah, it was," Lucy said. "If you could have seen your face, Leah!"

Megan didn't even care when, after the shop had emptied, Adrienne scolded her for teasing Leah. It wasn't much of a reprimand, and Megan could see that her mother was trying to restrain a smile.

It was Megan's turn to close the shop. Jade was off to the

library to meet Joseph, and Adrienne had a dinner date. Sophie and Lucy had evening baby-sitting jobs. Megan liked closing. It was so quiet in the shop when everyone else had gone. No more Pops yapping like puppies over this dress and that dress. And for Megan, no more feeling like she had two front teeth missing and a bad facial rash in the midst of all that perky perfection.

It was so much easier to be content with who she was when no one else was around.

She was halfway home when she remembered that she'd taken her chemistry book to the shop with her that morning, thinking she might slip in some study time. She hadn't, and finals were almost upon her. She was going to need that book. Might as well go back and get it tonight, since she was only halfway home.

Megan pulled the van into the alley near Quartet's side door. The courtyard was empty, the office building next door only dimly lit. Too early for people to be arriving at Impeccable Tastes, the upmarket restaurant on the ground floor of the office building.

She was almost at the shop's side entrance when something lying on the ground just outside the door caught her eye. There shouldn't have been anything there. She had swept around the door just before closing, as she always did, and fed a stray cat a saucer of milk, something her mother had expressly forbidden her to do. "Feed them," Adrienne said, "and they'll never leave. They can take care of themselves, Megan."

There hadn't been anything in the alley when Megan fed the cat.

But now there *was* something. A bundle of something lying in a puddle left over from the rain the night before. Wet newspapers, maybe.

Megan walked towards it. It wasn't newspaper, she realized as she got up close and looked down. It was . . . clothing. Crumpled and soaking wet with oily, muddy water. What looked like black tyre tracks were imprinted across the top layer.

Megan crouched to investigate the sodden mess.

Red . . . a red silk dress with spaghetti straps, one of them ripped away now, the dress so soaked with mud, the bright red had become dark brown. Beneath that, a black dress, strapless, its bouffant skirt flattened into a thick pancake by car tyres. And on the bottom in the fouled mess, something pale blue. . .

Leah's red prom dress. Zoe's black one. Beth's blue dress. Ruined, all of them, ruined beyond repair.

Megan knelt then, gingerly picking up the garments, holding the edges in her hands. No amount of steam cleaning or soaking or ironing would make them wearable again. They were beyond salvaging.

The ruined clothing clung to Megan's fingertips as if the dresses expected her to somehow miraculously restore them to their former glory. Frowning, Megan sank back on her heels.

What, exactly, had happened here?

Two

Megan had no idea how long she sat there on the cold, damp concrete, holding the remains of the slaughtered dresses in her hands. The sudden slam of a car door brought her head up. Glancing round the alley in search of someone who might look as if they had a psychotic hatred of fashion, she saw only a middle-aged couple heading towards Impeccable Tastes, the restaurant located directly ahead of Megan. She became aware of the tantalizing aroma of heavily seasoned Italian food. Her stomach smelled it too, and growled angrily.

I have to get up, Megan thought, her mind still foggy with shock. I have to get up and I have to do something about this mess. But she couldn't think what.

When she tried to swallow, her throat closed and she gagged.

It wasn't just the dresses that brought bile up into her

throat. Aside from the long hours her mother had put into making them, Megan didn't care about the garments. They were, after all, just dresses. And look who had purchased them: three girls who wouldn't lend you a shirt if you were standing naked in a snowstorm. Well, Beth or Zoe might. If Leah didn't talk them out of it.

It wasn't the dresses. It was the raw violence of the act that made Megan gag and sent her fingernails digging into the flesh of her palms. It was the stupid, needless, vicious act itself. The dresses hadn't arrived in the alley on their own. They'd been brought to the puddle by someone bent on destruction. *Why* would someone attack and drown three pretty prom dresses and then, just in case they might still be salvageable, flatten their corpses into fashion oblivion by grinding them into the mud like insects under a heavy boot heel?

It made no sense. But the anger of the acts, the fury represented by the ruined garments, made Megan's hands shake.

I have to get out of here, she told herself again. This time, she scrambled to her feet, dragging the dresses behind her with one hand. She headed first for the massive rubbish bin to her right, then changed her mind and aimed for the van instead. She wouldn't get rid of them. Not yet. Impossible to describe to her mother the condition in which she'd found the three dresses. The only way anyone would believe such a thing would be to see it with their own eyes. She had to take the murdered dresses home with her.

Megan hated the idea. She couldn't bear the thought of how her mother's eyes would look when she saw the remains of three of her loveliest creations.

I can't do this alone, she decided as she started the engine. I can't! Remembering then that her mother had had dinner plans and wouldn't be home yet, anyway, Megan drove straight to the library to find Jade and Joseph.

When they had finally accepted as reality the disgusting sight presented to them in the back of the van, Jade turned away from the muddy mess and said, "Whose are they? I can't even tell what colour they are . . . were."

Megan told her who had bought the dresses.

Jade's eyes and mouth opened wide. "The Pops? These dresses belong to the Pops?" A slow, satisfied grin spread across her face. "Oh, this is cool, this is just too cool! I don't believe this!"

"Jade," Megan said as she slammed shut the van's back door, "stop rejoicing and think about my mother, OK? She worked really hard on those dresses. This is going to make her even sicker than it made me. You guys have to come with me. I can't face her with this alone."

Jade's grin disappeared. Megan's remark had wiped every

last trace of exultation from her face. "Oh, no, you're right! I'm sorry! I wasn't even thinking about Adrienne. How are you ever going to tell her?"

"I'm not going to *tell* her anything. I'm just going to show her. I don't want to, but I have to. Those dresses are paid for. She'll have to do something about this. Get in. You're coming with me."

"Why would someone *do* this?" Adrienne cried, whirling to face Megan, Joseph, and Jade. "It's so . . . it's so . . . violent!"

"My thoughts exactly," Megan said grimly.

Then the businesswoman in Adrienne took over again. "Was the shop broken into? How did those dresses get outside? Was any money taken?"

Megan had to confess that she didn't know. "I found them in the alley and brought them here," she said, feeling stupid for failing to check the shop's doors and windows. Hadn't checked inside, either, to see if the culprit was still lurking there. "I guess I freaked out. I never even thought about the shop."

"I'd better get down there," her mother said, grabbing her jacket from the hall cupboard. "I can't call the police until I've checked out the shop. I'll call from there."

"You should call them first," Joseph suggested. "If there *was* someone in the shop, you can't be sure they've gone. You don't want to go walking in there alone."

Adrienne hesitated in the doorway. But after a moment, she shook her head. "I can't call the police and say that three prom dresses were ruined. We'll just go down and see if there's any sign of a broken lock or window. If there is, we won't go in, OK? We'll call the police."

"We?" Jade asked nervously, her eyes wide.

"She *said* we won't go inside." Megan glared at Jade. "Besides, we don't have to worry. *We're* not prom dresses. We don't even *own* prom dresses. So relax!" But even as she said it, she knew relaxing, for any of them, was impossible. It seemed amazing to her that they were walking and talking like normal people who hadn't seen what they had.

Because neither the front nor side door locks had been tampered with, they did go inside the shop. But they went slowly, cautiously, Adrienne leading the way with a torch until she reached the main light switch behind the counter.

Nothing seemed out of place. There was no pile of shredded garments lying on the floor, (something Megan had dreaded), no money missing, and nothing, inside the shop, as far as they could tell, had been broken or stolen.

Until they went upstairs to the sewing room they called the Sweatbox because it had no air-conditioning, and Megan discovered that the lock on the window leading from the fire escape was broken. "It was OK earlier today," she announced.

21

"I know, because I closed and locked the window when I came back in after my break."

The Sweatbox was a long, narrow room cluttered from ceiling to floor with bolts of fabric, sewing materials, large pink dress boxes, smaller pink boxes for shirts and tops and jumpers, thick packages of folded pale pink tissue paper, a huge cardboard box filled to overflowing with satin padded hangers, another filled with clear plastic hangers.

Half-finished dresses hung on armless plastic mannequins. An antique sewing machine inherited by Adrienne from the grandmother who had taught her how to design patterns and sew, stood against one wall. An old ironing board, part of the same inheritance, stood in the middle of the room. The board, its wooden legs old and wobbly, was constantly collapsing, but Adrienne refused to give it up. "It was my grandmother's," she insisted. "Without my grandmother, we wouldn't have the shop. I'd still be temping in an office by day and waitressing at night, like I did for eight very long years after your father raced that train at the crossing and lost. The ironing board stays."

There were two tall, narrow windows in the attic-like room, one overlooking a driveway, the other opening onto a black metal fire escape that rose above the courtyard outside the office building and restaurant.

That afternoon, when Megan had taken her break and

stepped out onto the fire escape to gulp in a few breaths of fresh air, her eyes had moved down to the restaurant and she had thought, people will be going there for their pre-prom dinner. The Pops would, in the beautiful dresses that Adrienne had created. But not Adrienne's own daughter.

And she had thought that if she *were* going, she knew exactly which dress she would want to wear. Not black, like Zoe. Black was for funerals. The dress she had fallen in love with when Adrienne was still creating it, was blue. The brilliant blue of an October sky at that time of the year when the nights turn crisp and the leaves turn orange and yellow and scarlet. Such a vivid shade of blue could turn even plain brown hair as glossy and smooth as a chestnut, give brown eyes a shining, golden glow. Megan was as sure the dress was miraculous as she was that she would never be wearing it. Not to the prom, and not anywhere else.

The thought had brought a sudden stab of pain to her chest, as if her mother had accidentally stabbed her with a sharp needle. The pain had made Megan angry, and thoroughly disgusted with herself. She hadn't realized, until that moment, just how much she wanted to go to her own senior prom.

And she'd suddenly been afraid that she was turning into one of those weepy, whining females who put *dances* at the top of their priority list. She hadn't attended a single prom at high school. And so far, she'd lived through every one of them, coming out on the other side of the weekend with all of her faculties intact and no visible serious damage.

But this was her *senior* prom.

"Are you sure that lock was intact this afternoon?" Adrienne's voice broke into Megan's thoughts.

Megan snapped out of it, turned round. "Yes, I'm positive."

Adrienne called the police to file a report, but the investigator found no clues to suggest anything more than youthful vandalism. Adrienne agreed.

Megan had her doubts. A band of young kids roaming the streets looking for prom dresses to ruin? Taking no money, breaking nothing, not even spray-painting the walls outside the shop? What were they doing in the shop in the first place? And why had they only destroyed those three dresses? Youthful vandalism? Reality check, please. There had been a purpose behind such selective sabotage.

Unfortunately, Megan couldn't even begin to imagine what that purpose had been.

If someone thought that wrecking those particular dresses would keep Zoe or Beth or Leah from the prom, they seriously needed a brain scan. Even if Adrienne couldn't replace them (and she *would*), there were other shops, other dresses. And lots, lots more money. Zoe's, Beth's, and Leah's mothers were the other owners of Quartet. They had invested money in Adrienne's shop because they had so much of it lying around doing nothing. Now, while they played tennis and gardened and enjoyed long lunches at Impeccable Tastes, and only Adrienne worked long, hard hours in the shop, their money grew. No, money was definitely not a problem when it came to replacing the three slaughtered dresses.

So if keeping the Pops from the prom wasn't the intent behind the violence, what was?

She was too tired to think about it now.

When the police had left, after instructing Adrienne to replace the broken lock, she asked Megan, Jade and Joseph to please keep the incident to themselves. "Bad for business," she said in a disheartened voice.

They all promised not to tell anyone.

In a heartier voice, Adrienne said, "I'll re-make the dresses. Megan, that might mean you'll be working longer hours in the shop. I'm sorry."

Refusing to think about exams coming up, which meant hitting the books in a major way, or senior activities like the picnic and Yearbook Day and the senior banquet, Megan nodded. "No problem." It wasn't as if she'd be busy getting ready for the prom.

When they left the shop, after making sure that

everything was locked up tighter than a bank vault, Megan's eyes avoided the puddle where the dresses had gone to their death. She carefully stepped around it, as if she were afraid that walking through it might bring her the same fate.

Three

The senior picnic was held on the following Wednesday, a grey, chilly day, threatening rain. Classes were suspended for all those who had made it to graduation without collecting more Fs than Bs. They travelled by car to the beautiful stretch of parkland north of Glenview known as Peninsula Point. Aptly named, the park was located in the very centre of a long, narrow strip of land stretching towards the ocean like a pointing finger.

While the peninsula's middle was lush with greenery, the tip itself was barren, the only colour provided by the golden-beige of windblown sand dunes and the white stone of an old, abandoned lighthouse.

A white metal sign on a rusted metal chain in front of the entrance to the lighthouse swung gently in the ever brisk ocean breeze, spelling *Danger* and warning visitors against entering the aging structure.

Many people ignored the sign. To some, the word Danger acted as a red flag, enticing them to climb over the chain and push open the rickety old door whose lock had been useless for years. To others, the thought of the awe-inspiring view from the circular wooden platform at the top of the structure just beneath the light itself, drew them onwards and upwards, heedless of the risk. The floor and wooden railing encircling the observation deck might be rotting and crumbling, but the spectacular view of the endless ocean remained intact. Nature lovers who made the precarious climb up the rusted metal spiral stairs that trembled beneath their weight felt the view was worth both the climb *and* the risk.

The small white metal sign continued to flap uselessly in the breeze as if to say, "Well, I tried my best. It's not my fault if they all ignore me."

Megan loved the lighthouse. She'd been making the shaky climb to the top since she was a child, Adrienne's stern warnings going unheeded. Few things were as thrilling to Megan as reaching the top, breathless, knees trembling from the climb, emerging through the small, weather-beaten door to the deck to step outside and face the broad, endless stretch of ocean and sky. She didn't mind the wind slamming into her like a cannonball, and she loved the taste of saltwater on her lips. Sometimes the water was grey-green, sometimes grey-blue. On cold, wind-whipped days, it was always grey-white, the waves taller than Megan.

It was like that on the day of the picnic, the ocean raging grey-white, every last trace of blue or green gone from the water, blanketed by a sooty grey sky overhead.

Still upset over the vandalism at the shop and tired of playing softball and volleyball, Megan left the festivities and trudged up towards the Point alone. No use asking Jade or the others to come along. Sophie and Lucy were afraid of the lighthouse, and Jade hated it, calling it a "creepy old relic that should have been torn down a long time ago". Megan knew she was just quoting her mother. Celia LaSalle, a close friend of Adrienne's, had no interest in the past, and called antiques "junk". She called the lighthouse "an eyesore to our community and a death trap".

Megan had never thought of the lighthouse as "a death trap". The only person who had ever died at the lighthouse, as far as Megan knew, was old "Suds" Crater, who was ancient himself and drank so much that people in town joked that he'd actually died a long time ago but the alcohol in his system had preserved him for all eternity. He had fallen from the observation deck on a warm, balmy night in October. The fall had literally scared him to death, Megan had heard. His heart had stopped on the way down.

When she finally reached the top of the lighthouse stairs,

Megan moved to the edge of the circular walkway, avoiding broken floorboards. The wind ripped the hood off her head and stung her eyes. Careful not to lean against the wooden, waist-high railing, she thrust her hands into the pockets of her bright blue hoody. The sound of the breakers crashing into the rocks below thundered around her, as if a storm were imminent. She loved that sound.

But it was so loud, that when a voice behind her said, "Awesome, right?" she almost didn't hear it. She turned to find a tall, broad-shouldered figure in a red hoody standing slightly behind her on her left. Because he was wearing his hood up, it took her a few seconds to place him. Then a gust of wind caught the hood and flung it backwards, setting free thick, dark hair.

Dan McGill. Zoe Buffet's sometime boyfriend. Hard to figure why one of the cutest guys at Glenview would put up with an on-again, off-again relationship. And he must be nice, too, because he was always getting elected to things.

What did he see in Zoe?

Oh, come on, Megan. Beauty, brains, popularity, for starters. And Zoe wasn't mean, like Leah. Not all the Pops could be mean, or they wouldn't be popular, would they?

Dan moved up to stand beside Megan. "Sort of gives you a chill, doesn't it?" he asked loudly over the pounding of the surf. "And I'm not talking about the weather."

Megan's tongue had had a stroke. It was completely paralysed. She was so conscious of how close he was, she could only nod silently. But she did turn her head to glance over at him. A great face. All strong bones and angles, and his eyes were a warm, spaniel-brown. He wasn't smiling, but he looked as if he might have just finished smiling or was about to do so again. She'd seen that face smiling, at school, when he didn't know she was watching. It was awesome.

Then he shocked her out of her sudden muteness by turning towards her to give her a long look before asking, "Aren't you Megan Dunne? Is everything OK now at Quartet? I heard you had some trouble over there."

Megan's jaw fell open. But she couldn't be sure if she was surprised because he knew about the vandalism at the shop or because he knew who she was. "No one is supposed to know about that," she said, tasting salt spray as she spoke. "My mother was hoping no one would hear about it."

"Oh, sorry. My brother Eddie was one of the cops that night. He felt really bad, said your mum seemed scared."

"She wasn't scared," Megan responded a bit sharply. "My mother's not afraid of anything. She was upset, that's all. Who wouldn't have been?"

He held up a defensive hand. "Hey, take it easy. I wasn't insulting her. Eddie just felt bad for her, that's all."

Had she heard the officer say his name was McGill? Megan didn't think so. If she had, she might have paid more attention to him. "It made all of us sick that the dresses were ruined. My mother worked really hard on them. And the prom isn't that far away now. Doesn't give her a whole lot of time to replace them." She couldn't believe she'd mentioned the prom. If he asked her who her date was, she'd have to utter the dreaded words, "I don't have a date".

Well, so what? It was the truth, after all.

So if he asked her, she would tell the truth. And she wouldn't lower her eyes or turn her face away, she'd just say it, straight out.

But he didn't ask. Instead, he leaned his elbows on the railing and to Megan's surprise said, "Me, I'm skipping the prom this time round." The railing's flaking white paint clung to the sleeves of his red hoody. "The old wallet's flat as a pancake."

Or flat as a dress run over by the tyres of a car, Megan thought darkly. Why had he reminded her of what had happened at Quartet? She'd been trying not to think about it, or about what it might mean.

She said nothing out loud. He wasn't going? One of the most popular guys at school wasn't going to his senior prom? He wasn't taking Zoe? But she'd bought a dress. Never mind that the dress was, literally, roadkill now. There would be a replacement in time. Adrienne would see to that. Had Zoe snubbed Dan for a college guy?

Or . . . delicious thought . . . maybe he hadn't *asked* Zoe. After all, she could afford to foot the bill, if he really wanted to go with her. Was he one of those stiff-necked guys who insisted on paying his own way? Whatever the reason, Dan McGill wasn't going to be escorting Zoe and her sexy black dress to Glenview's prom.

The sun suddenly seemed to be shining although, when Megan glanced up, the sky was that same solid slate-grey. It hadn't changed. So why did she suddenly feel much warmer?

Might as well spit it right out, Megan told herself and said, "You're not taking Zoe?"

"Zoe? Nope. Went with Zoe last year." His voice was noncommittal. "I heard she's going with some college friend of her brother Brandon." Still no inflection in his voice. He'd heard? He hadn't talked to Zoe lately? More good news. She couldn't help wishing that something in his voice would tell her if he cared that Zoe was going with someone else. But it didn't.

"You shouldn't lean on that railing," she warned. "It's too shaky. I don't want to have to climb around on those rocks down there picking up the pieces if that railing crumbles and takes you down with it."

Nodding agreement, he took a step backwards. "So, is the shop OK now? Haven't had any more break-ins, have you?"

"No." She wouldn't have minded talking about the incident with him. It would have been nice to bounce all her questions off someone who could be objective. Adrienne refused to discuss it, insisting that it had just been a prank and the police would handle it. Jade had been so frightened by the whole thing that her face went grey if Megan even mentioned it, and the only thing Joseph had on his mind these days was how to persuade Jade to invite him to the prom.

Even if the childish-prank theory had made sense to Megan, which it didn't, it wouldn't explain the deep, dark chill she felt when she remembered kneeling on that cold, damp concrete holding the remains of those dresses in her hands.

She had many, many questions about the ugly incident, and needed to talk them over with someone. But she couldn't talk to Dan about it. Adrienne would be very upset if she knew Megan was discussing the incident with anyone other than Jade or Joseph, who already knew.

The wind attacked them with a gust so fierce, it took Megan's breath away. "Everything's fine at Quartet," she said. "I need to go back now. I've been gone a long time. And I'm getting cold."

"Right. Me too."

She hadn't expected him to come with her. But she

couldn't help thinking how cool it would be if he walked all the way back to the picnic with her and they showed up at the park together. Jade would freak out. Unfortunately, the Pops would probably freak out, too. The Pops freaking out would not be a good thing.

Making up her mind to stay slightly ahead of Dan when they arrived at the park, Megan started down the circular metal staircase, stepping carefully and avoiding the rotting railing.

They descended them, their trainers making gentle slapping sounds on the steps. They passed no one. Megan wondered how Dan had known who she was. She wasn't wearing her Quartet badge, a small, silver piece made by joining together four tiny musical instruments: a violin, a clarinet, a viola, and an oboe. A friend of Adrienne's had designed them. She'd ordered hundreds of them to give away as souvenirs to customers. They sat in a wicker basket near the register. Anyone could take one.

But Megan wasn't wearing hers. Not that it would have told him much. It wasn't as if the badge spelled out her name. Tons of teenagers in Glenview owned one of those badges. But he'd said, "Aren't you Megan Dunne?" How had he known that? Maybe Zoe had pointed her out, mentioned that her mother ran Quartet.

Any other time, Megan would simply have asked. That

was the way she was. If a question was on her mind, she would blurt it out, fully expecting an answer. Sometimes that tactic got her into trouble, but so far, that hadn't stopped her.

But this felt different. Although her tongue had fully recovered, she couldn't quite make it ask, "How did you know who I was?" She wasn't sure why. Maybe because she was afraid he would say, "Zoe told me." She'd hate that. Yuck!

They were outside and on their way up the track towards the park when he answered the question for her. "Eddie was right," he said casually.

"Eddie? Your brother the cop? Right about what?"

"He said the woman who owns Quartet is gorgeous."

Megan nodded. It no longer pained her that she looked more like the pictures of her father than she did Adrienne. For years, she had just assumed that when she was old enough, she would look exactly like her mother. They had the same colouring. But the summer she was thirteen, she had suddenly spurted up to her full height and grown into her adult face. Then the truth was inescapable. She had inherited her mother's eyes. But that was all. She'd been furious, that whole summer and for most of the following school year. She couldn't remember now exactly when it had stopped making her angry. One day she had told herself that if she looked exactly like her mother, she might meet someone like her father. Then he might want to marry her and she might say OK. Then, one day when she thought everything was great, he'd get drunk because although he was cute and charming and tons of fun, he had never really grown up. He would try to race a train at a crossing, a really childish thing to do, and he'd lose. Then, like her mother, she'd be left alone, without any money, to raise any children they'd had.

The dismal, imagined scenario had gone a long way towards helping her be grateful for who she really was. Not to mention appreciating who her mother was and what she'd been through.

"She is gorgeous. You've seen her?"

"Nope. Never."

Puzzled, she glanced up at him. "Then how do you know your brother was right about what she looks like?"

Without returning her glance, he said very casually, "The second thing my brother said was that her daughter had the prettiest eyes he'd ever seen, including his wife Becky's. So, I figure, since I can see for myself that he was right about that, I know he had to be right about your mum being gorgeous, too. I'd like to meet her some time."

Caught off-guard by the roundabout way in which he'd told her she had nice eyes, Megan could only ask lightly, "Because she's gorgeous?"

He laughed. "No. Because Eddie said she was really nice."

Although the prom was still more than two weeks away, Megan felt like dancing right there on the dusty, rutted road. He wasn't going to the prom. Not with Zoe, not with anyone. And he had said she had nice eyes. And he was keeping up with her, stride for stride, so that Pops or no Pops, they were definitely going to be walking onto the picnic grounds together.

He's just being nice, she thought to herself. His brother told him about the demise of the dresses and he thought it was a shame, that's all. Don't go making this into something it isn't, Megan Dunne. That's just not like you.

She tried. She really did. But he was so nice, bending his head against the wind to ask her about the shop and her family and what she liked to do when she wasn't working at Quartet and had she played softball all her life because he'd been watching her play and was impressed with the way she hit the ball every single time, whacked it right out of the park almost and had she ever thought of playing in a summer league because he was going to and they could always do with new players.

It almost undid her when he talked about summer, as if there were no reason on earth why, come summer, they wouldn't still be walking like this and talking like this and even playing on the same softball team.

She was about to respond with something truly inane

like, "I just adore softball," something Megan Dunne would never, ever have said if she'd been in her right mind, when they heard the scream.

Four

The girl in yellow, wearing a matching print headband on her head, had no intention, on such a nasty day, of making the trek from the park to the lighthouse. For one thing, she knew the wind at the Point would absolutely destroy her hair, and she and her boyfriend were going to McDougal's at seven that night for burgers and dancing. She preferred Impeccable Tastes herself, like her parents, but he said it was too expensive, and he was nuts about burgers. Besides, she'd picked the restaurant the last three times and he was getting a little annoyed about that. Of course, he was getting annoyed about practically everything these days. If it weren't for the prom being so close, she'd have it out with him. He had no business treating her like yesterday's news.

She was *not* walking into McDougal's with her hair looking like she'd stuck her finger in an electric socket. Her headband would be useless in keeping her hair in place against the ferocious wind up at the Point.

But when someone came up to her just as she was leaving the ladies and whispered in her ear that her boyfriend had gone to the lighthouse with a cute, red-haired girl, what was she supposed to do? Pretend she didn't believe it? Of course she believed it. It wasn't the first time, was it? Not everyone knew she sometimes had trouble keeping him on a leash, especially lately. Truth was, she had actual nightmares that he dumped her two days before the prom, with her dress hanging right there in her wardrobe, and her hair appointment all set for Saturday morning at eleven. Even *she* wouldn't be able to dredge up a decent date in two days.

Everyone at school would laugh at her.

Any other time, she'd have dumped him so fast for the way he was treating her, he'd feel like he'd been tossed out of a plane without a parachute. But she couldn't, not now. Not this close to the prom.

Everyone said it was a dead cert she'd be queen. And even if she wasn't, which wasn't at all likely, she still didn't want to miss the prom.

She was convinced he already had a replacement in mind. She had no idea who it was, but imagined some stupid little bimbo holding her breath, waiting to see if the breakup would come in time for *her* to be taken to the prom by a gorgeous, popular senior.

It would never happen. Never! Not while she had a breath left in her own beautiful body.

"The lighthouse?" she asked, her head jerking up as if someone had punched her in the chest. "He took someone to the lighthouse?"

"Yes. You're not going to let him get away with it, are you?"

The girl in yellow hesitated. If she went after him, if she made a fuss, wouldn't she have to break their date for the prom? Was that what he was aiming for? Trying to make a fool of her here at the picnic so she'd lose her temper and give him an easy way out? Or . . . was it simple arrogance? Figuring he could get away with anything he wanted to because he was so sure she wouldn't want to break their prom date?

Well, he was right about that. He knew her so well.

Never*the*less. One person had already seen him take that bimbo, whoever she was, up to the lighthouse. Others could see him, too. Humiliating. She wasn't going to stand for that. Fortunately, the someone who *had* already spotted him had been kind enough to alert her. "No," she said, deciding. "I'm not going to let him get away with it. I hate that place, but I'm going up there."

"I'll come, too. Let's take the back way, through the woods to the beach. So he won't see us coming."

42

Because the ladies was hidden behind a grove of ash trees, no one saw the two leave the park.

Nor was there anyone at the lighthouse when, breathless because they had hurried, anxious to catch the faithless rat, they arrived at the lighthouse and went inside.

"They're probably already up on the observation deck," the girl in yellow was told.

"Right. Let's go. If he's stabbed me in the back again, I just might forget myself and give both of them one good, solid push against that disintegrating old railing. It would serve them right."

But it wasn't the faithless boyfriend who went over the edge of the observation deck, nor was it a conniving little bimbo with red hair.

Because there *was* no boyfriend in sight when the door was pushed open and the pair burst out onto the circular decking. There *was* no red-headed flirt. There was no one up there but the two girls who had hurried through the woods.

The girl in yellow turned to her companion. "Are you sure you saw him coming this way? He's not here." She sagged against the railing. It jiggled slightly in protest. "We shouldn't have come the back way. If we'd taken the road, we'd have caught them on their way back."

No reply. Just a cool, even stare.

The chill wind tugged at their clothing, at their hair, made their eyes water as they looked at each other. Then the girl's beautiful face fell. Her eyes narrowed as the truth dawned. "Oh, man, I don't believe this! I am such a fool. You never saw him coming up here with a girl! You never saw him coming up here at all. You made the whole thing up!" Perfectly arched brows drew together. "What for? Why would you say something like that when it wasn't true? It's so mean! I hate this place, I told you that. It's dangerous. What are we doing up here?"

The companion explained, slowly, measuring the words carefully, finishing with, "It's not so much to ask, is it? Such a little thing, really. How about it?"

The girl in yellow laughed. There was scorn in the sound. "That's the most ridiculous thing I've ever heard. Why would I do that?"

A head tilted, eyes went cold. "Because I asked you to. Because I need you to say yes."

"Not in this lifetime. That's crazy!"

The cold eyes narrowed. "Crazy? Crazy?"

"Well, it *is*. I would never agree to that."

"He *wants* to go with me. I wasn't going to tell you that. I was hoping I wouldn't have to. But he does. We've been . . . well, I've seen him a couple of times. When you were busy." A cool smile. "You *are* awfully busy, you know. He complains about that a lot. Anyway, he didn't have the guts to tell you

44

what was going on with us. He knew you'd go ballistic. He's such a coward. Look, I don't want him forever. Just for that one night. How can you be so selfish?"

A jaw dropped. "You? *You've* been seeing him? No, that's impossible. That's just as crazy as everything else you've said."

The voice dropped, became soft as a butterfly's wings. "It *was* me. Just say yes, OK? Just say you'll do this one tiny little thing for me. You can't care that much about him, or you wouldn't have ignored him the way you did. Your activities wouldn't have been more important than he was. So let him go, just for this one night. *He* won't break your date. No guts. *You* have to do it."

"Never. I'm not missing the prom. Everyone thinks I'll be queen this year. How can you even ask that?"

In that same butterfly-wing voice, "Oh, but you are missing the prom. One way or the other, you *are*." A foot stamped petulantly on the rotted wooden floor. "Why are you making this so hard? It was supposed to be *easy*."

Alarmed by the look in the eyes regarding her, the girl in yellow took a step backwards. But she remained defiant. "You are really insane, you know that?" Her first mistake.

"*Don't* say that again!"

"I . . . I didn't mean it. But I *am* going to the prom. Of course I am."

"*Oh, are you?* I don't *think* so."

The girl's eyes narrowed. Her voice was cold and remarkably unshaken as she said, "I don't know what your problem is, but I'm going back down. Right now. Let me pass!" Her defiance was her second mistake. But then, she was quite used to getting her own way.

"I can't do that. Not until you promise. Promise me you'll break your date with him, so he can take me. Do that, and I'll let you leave."

The girl in yellow, finally accepting that she was in real danger, instinctively took another step sideways. In her sudden fear, she forgot about the decrepit, weather-beaten railing. Her third mistake.

The instant her side slammed against it, the section of the railing gave way, crumbling like stale bread. Unprepared, she lost her balance and tumbled sideways, off the edge of the deck. She made no sound beyond a small, startled gasp. At the very last second, one well-manicured, ring-laden hand flew out and clutched a post.

Above her, hands flew to a mouth open in shock and horror. The fall, clearly not part of the plan, had created in the observer a frozen helplessness that did the victim no good at *all*.

The girl in yellow dangled by one hand, legs kicking frantically against the solid white stone of the lighthouse, her free hand clawing wildly at the wall for something to hang onto, seeking something substantial to clutch. "Help me!" she cried. "Please, help me!"

The figure standing on the deck above her immediately sank to her knees to lend a helping hand, crying, "Hold on, hold on, don't fall, I'll get you, hold on!" Both hands reached out, bent down. . .

And then pulled backwards slowly, as the shock and horror left the face and were replaced by something very different. "What am I doing? Why am I helping you? You wouldn't help me. I begged you, and you said no. You said I was crazy." The figure sank back on her heels, hands in her lap, eyes staring down into the face of the dangling girl. The girl in yellow's eyes were so full of terror, they should have melted even the hardest of hearts.

But they didn't. "No, no, I just don't think it would be right for me to help you," the voice said slowly, thoughtfully. "You can understand that, can't you? I mean, you weren't being the least bit cooperative. Not the least bit." The voice gathered speed. "And the thing is, it's not my fault you fell. I never touched you. It's not my fault, right?"

The horrified shock on the face of the girl's only hope of rescue had slowly but clearly turned into something very different. Slowly, gradually, the look in the eyes staring down at the white-faced victim clawing at the lighthouse wall, legs still now because kicking made it harder to support her weight, became that of a fox who has unexpectedly trapped its prey and is surprised by its good luck. A look of cold cunning. That look, in turn, changed again, became undisguised delight. Or, more accurately, maniacal glee at such good fortune.

The girl in yellow watched the face changing and her last shred of hope died. She knew then that she was going to do the same. She was going to die. Now. Right now. Because the face of the only person who could save her from plunging down upon those cruel, jagged rocks directly beneath her, a face that only moments ago had been white with shock and terror, was no longer quite human. Every shred of decency, of kindness, of forgiveness, of compassion, was gone, replaced by the unmistakable look of a predator.

And what she thought then was, I will get no help from such a face.

The figure above her stood up. The black, pointed tip of a shoe moved forward, ever so slightly and, nudging gently, began uncurling the fingers clutching the post. One finger left the post. Two. . .

"It wasn't my fault. I never touched you. You just fell, that's all."

The girl was not petite. The body that looked so perfect in jumpers and skirts, designer jeans and T-shirts, and formal dresses, was too substantial to be supported by a mere three-finger grip when gravity was tugging at it with great force.

48

The figure still on the deck suddenly reached down and snatched away the yellow headband the girl was wearing, and pocketed it. Then she straightened up and the toe slid forward one more time. "I *am* sorry, though. But you should have been more careful."

"No," the girl whispered, tears of anguish streaming down her face, streaking her make-up, "no, please, I'll do what you asked, I won't go to the prom, I won't. . ."

"Liar." The tip of the shoe pulled back and swung forward, hard, aiming at the remaining three fingers. It connected with a crunching sound and the hand slid free. The girl fell down, down, upon the wet, salt-sticky rocks below.

She screamed once on the way down, a helpless, hopeless shriek of terror.

"You were right." The voice sounded different now. "This place *is* dangerous."

As the figure turned away from the railing, a small object fell from her pocket. She bent to pick it up, then changed her mind and nodding, let it lie, half hidden beneath a worn wooden bench.

Then the shoe that had kicked out at the hand turned with its mate and the pair of them made their way back down the circular staircase, in no particular hurry.

Five

*S*he's dead. Dead! It's not what I planned and I didn't mean it to happen but it did and it wasn't my fault and I can't stop thinking that maybe now I'll get what I want. What she wouldn't give me.

It was so easy.

What am I going to do?

I can't stop shivering, and it's not even that cold down here. The wind can't get inside. No one can see me here, hiding in this place, can they? They won't look for me here, will they?

They won't look for me at all. Won't be looking for anyone, because when they find her, they'll think it was an accident. No one knows I was with her. I'm the only one alive who knows what happened, and I'm not telling. Not ever.

When they find her, I'll go back out then. I'll leave my hiding place and join the crowd that will come flocking down to the water to see what's happened. They'll think I was with them all the time, that I never left the picnic.

I'll have to be very careful to act like all the others. If they cry, I'll cry. If they don't, I won't. Just like them, I'll act just like them. No one will notice anything weird about me, I'll make sure of that.

But I feel weird. I feel so weird. But look how it's turned out for me. Better than I thought. I think . . . I think that if this doesn't work out the way I want, and it might not because sometimes things don't, I could do this again, and again, and again, until I do get what I want. It's so easy. Easy to make things look accidental. And no one would ever suspect me. I'm much too clever for that.

That look on her face . . . I'll see that in my dreams, maybe even while I'm awake, for the rest of my life. And I'll hear that scream even when I'm listening to music or taking part in a conversation or cheering at a ball game. It will ring in my ears as if it were happening at that very second instead of in the past.

I shouldn't punish myself like that. It really wasn't my fault. She should have been more careful. And I certainly couldn't help her after she refused to help me. That wouldn't have been right. Not right at all.

But she's dead. Gone. Forever. Out there in the water somewhere, floating like a bright yellow buoy.

There, the shivering has stopped. Because I feel strong now. Stronger than I ever have. I can do anything. I can have what I want.

And now I have a date for the prom.

Six

On the rutted road across the park, the scream stopped Megan and Dan in their tracks. The chilling sound married the whistling of the wind and became an eerie, anguished wail that faded as quickly as it had begun.

The two stood in wary silence. Across the road in the park, a raucous softball game stirred up dust. Spectators screamed and shouted, urging on their team. Some distance behind them, a more frenetic volleyball game was taking place. More shouting, more screaming. Megan waited for all of the players to stop what they were doing and listen to see if the wail of hopeless terror came again. It didn't. Had none of them heard the awful sound?

Dan was the first to speak. "What was that?" His voice was low, his dark head tilted slightly as if he were still listening.

Megan's heart resumed its beating. "I don't know."

The sharp crack of a bat sounded from the park. The

screams that filled the air then as the runner flew from home plate to first base and then on to second seemed, to Megan, very unlike the one they'd heard a moment earlier. That had sounded anything but playful to her.

But Dan's body relaxed and he said, "Oh, *that's* what it was! The game. Whew, had me going there for a minute. Sounded like someone having their worst nightmare, didn't it?"

And for just a moment, it was such a relief to be presented with a harmless, even comforting explanation for the bone-chilling shriek, Megan tried very hard to believe that he was right.

But she knew, somewhere deep inside her, that he was wrong.

"Yes, it did sound like someone's nightmare," she said, turning round to face the Point. "And it didn't come from the ball games." She pointed towards the lighthouse. "It came from there."

"Are you sure?"

"Positive." Dread sounded in her voice. "We have to go and check."

Someone shouted at Dan just then, urging him to join the game.

Megan saw him hesitate. He didn't really agree that the scream had come from the Point, and she could tell that he would much rather play ball than return to the lighthouse to investigate.

"I can go back by myself," she said, and began walking. Fast. Almost running. If she was right about where the scream had come from, she was probably also right that it meant something terrible.

Dan was beside her in seconds. Didn't argue with her, didn't tell her she was nuts, just ran along beside her. Megan felt a little better. She wasn't anxious to return to the lighthouse alone if there was trouble there.

They were halfway there when Jade stepped out of the woods, her hands filled with wild flowers already beginning to wilt. When Megan told her where they were going and why, she said, "I didn't hear any scream. You can ask Lucy and Joseph when they get here. They're in the woods somewhere, too."

"We're not waiting," Megan said urgently. "You can, if you want. Bring them to the lighthouse when they get here, just in case. We might need help."

"You're probably getting all upset over nothing," Jade bent her head to sniff the bouquet in her hands. "Could have been someone screaming at the park. It's a *picnic*, Megan. People scream when they're having fun."

But Megan was already running again, this time faster. Dan was right behind her.

They found nothing in the lighthouse. Their footsteps

echoed hollowly up the metal stairs, and although they repeatedly called out, no one answered them.

And when they reached the observation deck, it, too, was empty, occupied only by the whistling wind.

They were about to leave when Megan noticed that a top section of the railing was gone. "Dan? Look, the railing is broken."

"That railing's been rotting for years."

"I know it has. But this part of it wasn't broken just a little while ago, when we were up here. Come and look."

"You're right," Dan agreed. "This piece wasn't gone. I know, because this is where I leaned my elbows, until you told me not to. Must have fallen off after we left."

Footsteps pounding up the metal stairs signalled the arrival of Joseph, Jade and Lucy. When the door opened and the three joined Megan and Dan, Megan showed them the missing railing section.

"So it fell off after you left," Joseph suggested. His face was wet with sea spray, his red hair wild.

"Maybe." Careful not to lean against the rickety railing, Megan peered over its edge. The others did the same.

They all saw it at the same moment. Far below, floating in the churning, foaming water as it pounded up against the rocks, a yellow long-sleeved jacket, the back and sleeves water-laden, puffed up like balloons.

They were too far above it to see any more than that.

"It's just a jacket," Jade said nervously, backing away from the railing as if she expected it to attack her. "That's all it is, just a jacket."

"Probably," Dan agreed. "Can't tell from here. But we'd better go down and check."

Megan could tell from his voice that he wasn't convinced Jade was right.

It was impossible to go down those shaky stairs quickly. The descent seemed to take forever, as if someone were continually adding additional stairs as they moved downwards.

When they emerged into sunlight, Jade said, "I'm not going down there. To the water. I know it's just a jacket, of course it is. But you guys go and look. I'll wait here, OK?"

"I'll stay with you," Lucy said hastily.

Leaving them standing beside the stone steps, Dan, Joseph and Megan hurried along the rough, uneven ground and down a path leading to the beach.

Megan's heart was drumming unevenly in her chest. Jade was probably right. There couldn't be anyone inside that jacket being buffeted by the rough waves and the rocks. Because if there were, that person couldn't possibly be alive. The possibility of someone from the picnic being . . . dead . . . was something Megan wasn't willing to face.

The climb down the path was a difficult one. The ground was uneven and rocky, and wind and salt spray battled them every inch of the way. As they neared the spot where they had seen the jacket, giant waves crashing into the huge boulders lying at the edge of the water cascaded upwards and out, drenching all three of them. Megan's hair and face were soaked and sticky with salt.

Please, she prayed, stepping carefully, please don't let anyone be inside that floating jacket. Let Jade be right, please.

They finally made it to the edge of the water.

And Megan could see, then, that Jade was not right.

The shiny yellow jacket was not empty.

Someone was still wearing it.

Seven

"Oh, God," Megan whispered as the three stood at the water's edge staring in shock and disbelief. "It's Leah. It's Leah Markham." She knew it even before she saw the long, tangled mass of dark hair splayed out like seaweed round the head that bobbed, face up now, among the thunderous waves. "That's her yellow jacket."

The trio stood, paralysed with horror, on the rocky ledge, assaulted by a constant spray of salt water and the tugging of the angry wind. Their eyes were riveted to the spot in the churning, silvery waves where Leah Markham's left ankle was firmly imprisoned in a narrow crevice between two huge rocks.

After what seemed like hours, Joseph said to no one in particular, "If her foot wasn't stuck between those boulders, she'd be out to sea by now."

Dan and Megan made no reply.

Although the force of the water had washed away whatever blood there had been, sparing them at least that, there didn't seem to be a single facial bone left intact. The smooth olive features so admired at Glenview High had puddled into a boneless mass of sodden flesh. Had that not been Leah Markham's yellow jacket, had that not been her dark hair, none of the three could possibly have been certain *who* it was being buffeted by the rough, wind-driven waves like refuse from a shipwreck.

Her eyes were wide open. If her head had not been turned slightly towards the shore, she would have appeared to be gazing up at the sky. Instead, the glassy, doll-like stare led directly to the very top of the lighthouse.

All three heads turned automatically to follow Leah's sightless gaze.

"She fell from there." Dan wasn't asking a question. He was making a statement.

Megan nodded. "The broken railing. That," she sucked in her breath, "was the scream we heard. Leah falling." Shuddering, she turned away from the lighthouse.

"I don't get it." Dan continued to stare at the white tower. "Leah would never have gone up there alone. She hated the place. Anyway, she never went anywhere alone."

"Well, she couldn't have been with anyone," Joseph argued. "They would have helped her. Run to the park and brought people back to save her. Something. No one did that."

"I know that." Dan wiped salt spray from his face with his sleeve. "I'm just telling you, I've known Leah all my life, and she would never have gone up into that lighthouse alone."

Jade came up behind them so quietly, all three jumped when she asked in a tremulous voice, "Was I right? I was, wasn't I? It's just a jack. . ." Then she, too, saw. She let out a sickened cry. "Oh, no, who *is* it?"

"Leah Markham," Megan was the first to say.

"Is she . . . is she . . . ?"

Of course she was. How could she possibly still be alive? "Yes. She's dead." Megan turned to Dan. "We have to do something. We have to get her out of there."

"No." Dan wiped salt spray from his face with the back of his hand. "I don't think we should touch her. We have to leave her just as she is until the police arrive."

"The police?" Jade squeaked. "You mean an ambulance."

"I mean the police," Dan insisted. "She's dead, Jade. And it looks as if she fell from the deck, but I'm telling you, as a close friend of hers, that she would never have gone up there alone. So, it's time to call the police. Eddie says if you ever find a body and you don't know exactly what happened, don't touch it."

61

Jade turned her back to the water and began crying quietly. "We shouldn't leave her there, it's not right."

Dan nodded grimly. "I don't like leaving her there any more than you do, but she's already dead, Jade. You and Joseph go and make the call. Megan and I will stay here. Where's your friend? Lucy?"

Jade waved backwards. "Up there. She wouldn't come."

When Jade and Joseph had hurried away, Megan said quietly, "I'm sorry, Dan, but I can't stay and watch what's happening to her out there. She keeps slamming up against those rocks. It's making me sick. It's horrible!" Megan's voice broke. "But I don't want to leave her, either. What if we left and her foot slid loose? She'd float out to sea." She shuddered again, this time at the thought of Leah lost forever to a deep, dark, watery grave.

"You go and sit up at the lighthouse," Dan offered. "I'll stay here. Go on. When Jade and Joseph come back, they'll bring everyone from the picnic with them. Then it'll be your job to keep Michael from going off the deep end. If he hasn't already been told what's happened, break it to him gently, OK? He and Leah had their problems, but they've been going out since ninth grade."

Megan sat on the stone steps at the bottom of the lighthouse with Lucy, both of them trembling with cold and shock, trying to take in the horrible thing that had happened.

Megan was praying that Jade and Joseph would tell Michael. Please, please, she prayed, let someone else tell Michael so I don't have to. Please!

"I couldn't tell him," Jade whispered hastily to Megan as she and Joseph, breathless and red-faced, arrived back at the lighthouse, followed by a throng of picnickers curious about what was happening. "I don't even *know* Michael Danz, Megan. Let Dan tell him. They're friends."

But there was no way that Megan could lead Michael down to Dan, at the water's edge, and let Leah's boyfriend see what they had seen. Instead, she pulled him over to the side, away from the others, and broke the news as gently as she could. Then, when the awful news finally sank in and he tried to break away from her, she clutched at his left elbow and shouted to David, Lily's boyfriend, and Beth's boyfriend, Jordan, to help her keep Michael away from the water.

When they had quieted him down, Megan said gently, "You mustn't go down there, Michael. You can't help Leah now. I'm sorry. I am really sorry. She must have fallen from the lighthouse deck. There's a piece of the railing missing."

Michael snapped out of his shock enough to shout, "No! She wouldn't have gone up there! She hated that lighthouse, and she would never, never have gone up there alone! Why *would* she?"

Exactly what Dan had said.

No one had an answer to Michael's question.

Little by little, the dreadful news made its way through the crowd. Megan told Sophie. She, too, was intent on joining Dan at the water's edge. Megan stopped her. "You don't want to see," she said.

It seemed to her, as word circulated through the crowd, that everyone wanted to see. It took all her persuasive powers to keep them, especially Leah's closest friends, from hurrying down to the water. She and Jordan kept repeating that there was nothing they could do, but more important, they'd be in the way when the ambulance arrived. "Jade and Joseph will go down and stay with Dan," she concluded. "Could the rest of you please stay here with Michael?" She was afraid that if anyone left, Michael would follow.

"*I'm* not going back down there," Jade protested. Her face was as white as Michael's, and she was trembling. "I can't. It's . . . it's too awful."

Joseph went by himself.

Michael's friends rallied round him then, leading him to the stone steps and sitting with him while they waited for help to arrive. "She wouldn't have gone up there alone," he kept repeating. "She wouldn't have."

He said it so often, sometimes crying it out loudly, other times shaking his head and muttering the words to himself, that Megan became convinced that he and Dan were right.

Both knew Leah well. Could they be that wrong about what she would or wouldn't do? They seemed so certain.

On an impulse, she got up from the steps she'd been sitting on with Sophie, Sarah and Lucy, and moved to one side of the lighthouse, signalling to Zoe and Beth to join her. They looked dazed, their faces stony-white, their eyes blank.

"Megan?" Zoe asked dully as they arrived at her side. "Michael needs us now. What do you want?"

"You were Leah's best friends. Both of you. Is Michael right about how she hated the lighthouse?"

"Oh. Yes, he's right." Salt spray had completely undone Zoe's make-up and her blonde waves. Her hair hung limply along her shoulders like a wet scarf.

"Then what was she doing up there?"

Beth answered first. "I've been thinking about that." Her voice was husky with tears. "And I agree with Michael. I can't figure it out. This isn't the first time we've all been out here on the Point. We've been coming out here for years, having picnics and bonfires."

Megan nodded. "Us, too. I mean, my friends and I."

"Well, in all that time, Leah only went up into the lighthouse once. She hated it, said she would never go inside again. And as far as I know, she never did." Fresh tears shone in her blue eyes. "Until now."

Lily, seeing them gathered together, left the steps to join

65

them. She caught enough of the conversation to say to Megan, "Why are *you* so interested?" Her tone was hostile. "You're not a friend of hers. *We* are. We're her best friends, have been practically forever. Leah and Zoe and Beth and I. But not *you*. You hardly knew her."

"Lily, Megan's just trying to help," Zoe said.

But Megan thought the question was fair. She just didn't know how to answer it. She couldn't say, I'm interested because I've had this awful feeling in the pit of my stomach ever since I came across those slaughtered dresses at Quartet, and what's happened to Leah has made that feeling much worse. She couldn't say that, because her mother didn't want Zoe and Beth to know what had happened to their prom dresses.

Not that there could be any connection between the two disasters. How could there be? It would be stupid to compare the ruination of clothing to the brutal death of a real, live human being. It was just that the feeling she had now, right this minute, was like the feeling she'd had in the alley at Quartet, only magnified a million times because that corpse out there in the ocean, and she knew it *was* a corpse, had been a real, living, breathing human being, not something made out of fabric.

When Megan didn't answer, Zoe turned and went back to the lighthouse steps to console Michael. Beth, pressing a tissue to her eyes, followed.

Just because I didn't know the girl, Megan thought, turning to look down the slope towards Dan and Joseph, doesn't mean I'm not every bit as horrified as everyone else who did know her. Michael's face was ashen and his teeth were chattering with shock, and Beth was crying quietly. Zoe and Lily seemed intent on comforting Michael. David and Jordan, their faces sombre, waited silently for help to arrive, keeping their eyes on Michael.

Only Lucy said stubbornly, "Don't expect me to burst into tears, Megan, because it's not going to happen." She was clearly remembering Leah's cruel remarks at Quartet. Her own remarks were almost a whisper, which Megan was grateful for. "I couldn't stand that girl and I'm not going to pretend I'm shattered. She was mean, you know she was."

"Not mean enough to die like that," Megan whispered back, seeing that grotesque, ruined face again. Ruined . . . like the dresses in the alley. But . . . this was a *life* ruined. Gone. Destroyed.

Not something Adrienne could fix with a needle and thread. Not this time.

Eight

The ambulance came first, stopping with a startling shriek of brakes. Paramedics on board donned wet suits to retrieve the victim from the cold, rough waters. A police car arrived almost simultaneously. Two officers got out and made their way down the slope to where Dan and Joseph were still standing.

Megan gave Jordan and David a lot of credit for their ability to hold Michael back. He wanted desperately to run down to the water, but the two boys wouldn't let him. They had to physically restrain him, talking to him in urgent tones, until he sank down on the top step in defeat, all the fight drained out of him. Once, Megan thought she heard him murmur, "It's my fault, it's all my fault," but she knew she must have misunderstood. Michael had been playing ball when that scream sounded. He hadn't been anywhere near the lighthouse.

The wait seemed to stretch on forever. Only the sun poking in and out among the clouds provided a smattering of warmth from time to time. They had inadvertently divided into two slightly separate groups, the larger group, Michael surrounded by his friends, the other, Megan and her friends. They huddled there, trying to keep warm, anxiously awaiting some sound, some signal that Leah Markham was no longer being brutally battered against the rocks.

The tension was broken first by the sound of voices approaching from behind the lighthouse.

The group on the steps stood up, all faces filled with dread except Michael's. Megan could tell, when she glanced at him, that he was still holding out hope. Because he hasn't seen what I saw, she realized. He still doesn't believe she's dead.

The two policemen appeared round the corner of the lighthouse first, immediately followed by a rubber-suited paramedic carrying a stretcher. On it lay a black plastic body bag, carefully zipped completely shut. A second man in a wet suit was holding the other end of the stretcher.

It was a sight no one standing on the lighthouse steps would ever forget. The black zippered bag told the whole story. Leah Markham had not survived that cold, battering surf. It wasn't even likely that she had survived the fall from the deck.

Michael let out a sound and dropped to the steps, his head in his hands. Beth and Lily burst into tears. Zoe muttered something and leaned against the building, her hands over her mouth. Jordan and David stared silently at the gruesome body bag, as did Sophie and Lucy.

Dan and Joseph trailed behind the stretcher, their faces grim.

While the stretcher was loaded into the ambulance, the two officers approached the group frozen on the steps. One policeman whipped out a small notebook and a pen. He was kind enough to wait until the ambulance departed before saying, "Sorry, folks, but I'm going to have to ask a few questions here. Anyone see what happened to that girl?"

The second officer made his way through the group, yanked open the lighthouse door, and disappeared inside. His heavy footsteps clanking up the metal stairs echoed in the cool air.

The officer still outside took names, telephone numbers, then asked each person if they had seen or heard anything.

Only Dan and Megan had heard the scream.

The officer asked what time they had heard it, and then jotted down the time. Then he asked each of them where they had been at that time.

Megan wasn't really listening to the answers. She couldn't get the sight of that black rubber body bag out of her mind. She was vaguely aware of answers like, "Picking flowers in the woods", "hiking along the north shore", "playing volleyball", "in the ladies", "in the car-park", even, "I dunno, just sitting, I guess", but wasn't aware of which person gave which answer. It didn't really seem to matter.

Unashamed tears slid down Michael's face. "Are you the boyfriend?" the officer asked, moving to stand in front of Michael. "Were you up there with her when she fell?"

"No. If I had been, I wouldn't have let her fall." Michael sounded angry.

"How come you weren't with her?"

Megan stared at the policeman. Good question. She would never have thought of asking it. But she had never, ever seen Leah Markham alone. If she hadn't been with her three best friends, she'd been with Michael. At school, at the mall, at the cinema, at dances and parties. There were rumours that he wasn't the most faithful person in the world, but they'd never ended the relationship. So why *wasn't* he with her when she climbed those lighthouse steps?

Michael didn't answer right away. The officer had to ask the question a second time. "I . . . we . . . we had a fight. I mean," Michael added hastily, "not a *real* fight. Just a little

71

argument, really. I wanted to play softball and she didn't. Said she'd get all sweaty. She got angry and took off. I played, and when the game was over, I went looking for her. Couldn't find her. Then that girl," pointing to Jade, "came running into the park saying something terrible had happened. I knew right away she meant Leah. Because Leah hadn't come back."

"A fight?" It struck Megan that the officer hadn't heard a single word after that first sentence. "You fought with the dead girl?"

At the phrase "dead girl", everyone in the group shuddered. They were nowhere near ready to think of Leah Markham as "the dead girl".

"It wasn't a *fight*," Michael persisted. Megan thought she heard fear in his voice. She'd be scared, too, the way that policeman pressed for answers.

Everyone knew Leah and Michael had argued a lot. Big deal. That didn't mean he'd pushed her off the top of a lighthouse.

Pushed? The thought stunned Megan. No one had said that Leah was *pushed*. The railing had broken while she was leaning on it, and she'd fallen to the rocks below, that was all. Wasn't it?

Oh, Megan, her inner voice said, you don't believe that for a second. You never did. Not after Dan and Michael told you

72

Leah wouldn't have gone up to the lighthouse alone. Isn't that why your stomach is in such turmoil?

No, Megan argued with herself, no! That's not true. I don't *want* that to be true, any of it. It's too horrible.

But she hadn't convinced her stomach. It continued to churn like the waters that had trapped Leah.

The second officer emerged from the lighthouse, holding something up in the air for his partner to see.

Megan couldn't see what it was. It didn't look very big. It seemed, in the dim light, to be shiny and small. An earring? Something of Leah's?

She took a step closer. Her eyes, like everyone else's, were on the object in the officer's hand.

It was a badge. A small, silver badge, four musical instruments joined together to create a quartet. Quartet. It was one of the badges Adrienne gave away as souvenirs at the shop so that "our customers won't forget us".

"Anyone know whose this is?" the officer asked. "I found it up there on the floor, right next to the railing."

Megan frowned. She had never, not once, seen Leah Markham wearing one of the Quartet badges. She wore only gold jewellery. Very expensive gold jewellery. She might have taken one of the souvenirs, just because they were there, but she would never have been caught dead . . . she would never have worn it.

"Oh, we all have those," Beth said, her voice still choked with tears. "They give them away at Quartet. Everyone in town has one."

Yes, Megan thought, but not everyone wears them. Leah wouldn't have.

She said so then, out loud. "Leah wouldn't have worn one of those badges. She only wore gold jewellery. Right, Michael?"

He looked blank for a moment, and then his expression cleared, and he nodded. "Right. Gold. She didn't like the cheap stuff. Wouldn't wear it."

"So that's not hers," Megan told the officer. "It's someone else's. And. . ." She hesitated. When she spoke again, she was really only thinking aloud. "The first time I was up on the deck this afternoon," she mused slowly, thoughtfully, "that badge wasn't there. I would have noticed it. My mother runs the shop that gives them away, and I work there, so the badges mean a little bit more to me than they would to someone else. If one had been lying on the deck, I would have noticed."

The officer looked sceptical. 'Maybe you're so used to seeing these badges all the time, one could have been right under your nose and you wouldn't have paid any attention."

"That's probably true when someone's wearing one," Megan agreed. "I guess I don't always notice when a badge is on a shirt or jumper or blazer. But if one had been lying at my feet when we were up on that observation deck, I would have bent and picked it up, the same way I would in the shop. It wasn't there, officer."

One grey, bushy eyebrow lifted. 'We? I thought you said *you* were up there. Sounded like you meant alone."

Megan felt her cheeks redden. "I was alone, at first. But then, he came up," pointing half-heartedly to Dan, wondering if he'd be angry that she'd brought him into the discussion, "so I wasn't alone when I came back down."

"You and Dan?" Beth asked, astonishment in her voice. "At the lighthouse?"

Megan felt all eyes on her. She knew her face was flushing, and felt defensive. Since when was it a crime to run into someone on the observation deck?

The officer turned his attention to Dan. "Did you see anything?"

"No, sir."

"You didn't notice the badge lying on the deck?"

"No. But it could have been there. It's pretty small. It probably wouldn't have caught my eye. I wasn't looking at the floor."

"There must have been a lot of people up there today," Joseph interjected. "What with the picnic and all. That badge could belong to anyone, like Beth said."

A tearful Beth nodded. So did the police officer.

End of story, Megan thought. And he was probably right. The badges were so commonplace. Anyone could have dropped one. But she was still convinced that it had been dropped sometime between her first trip up there and her second.

"You kids aren't supposed to come near this place," the officer said sternly. "Can't you read that sign? It's there for a reason." He shook his head. "Takes a terrible tragedy like this, a fatal accident, before you people take warnings seriously. Think you're invincible, but you're not. I guess you know that now, right?"

When they were allowed to leave, they walked in a stunned silence up the road towards the car-park, anxious by now to get as far away from the Point, the lighthouse, and the park as possible.

Megan, walking between Joseph and Jade, tried to focus on the officer's lecture. "A fatal accident", he had said. She wanted to believe that, more than anything. But everyone who knew Leah kept insisting that she wouldn't have gone to the lighthouse alone. Or gone up the stairs to the observation deck. And there was that badge. If Leah hadn't been wearing it, who had?

Megan wanted to stop thinking about it, but she couldn't. Her mind raced onwards without her permission, a rebellious child out of control. What if Leah *hadn't* gone up there alone? What if she'd gone up there *with* someone?

Then that someone would have helped her, would have kept her from falling somehow. And if they'd failed and she'd fallen anyway, they'd have come racing back up the road to the park to shout for help, like Joseph had said. They would have reported the accident.

But no one had done that.

Megan felt a chill that had nothing to do with the temperature.

Impossible that someone could have witnessed that fall to the rocks and done nothing. Someone like that would have to be totally, completely, heartless. No . . . worse than that. Someone like that would have to be totally, completely, sick. How else could someone watch what had happened to Leah on those rocks and then return to a picnic to eat hot dogs and drink Coke and play volleyball or softball and laugh and talk, just as if everything were as normal as it had always been? It wouldn't have been for long, because Joseph and Jade must have come racing back to the park shortly after Leah fell. But still . . . how could someone *do* that, even for a short while?

The image was so sick, it made Megan dizzy. Her head ached fiercely. Either there had been no one on that observation deck when Leah fell to her death, which was what Megan wanted fiercely to believe, or there *had* been someone there. Because Leah would never have gone up there alone.

If there *had* been someone up there, Megan didn't want to think about how sick or evil that person had to be.

Nine

L ike it or not, everyone had to return to the park to gather up their belongings and do a hasty clean-up.

Megan, hurriedly tossing dirty paper plates into a large black plastic bag, thought the people around her looked like robots. Their movements were slowed, their bodies moving stiffly, as if they'd been mechanically programmed. The expression on every face was one of numbed shock. No one spoke. Every last trace of party atmosphere was gone. In its place, Megan decided, was something very different. The word that came to mind sounded the same, but was spelled differently. Atmos*fear*. They were all afraid.

Even me, she realized. That one of them could die so suddenly, so horribly, had shattered every single person who had known Leah Markham, no matter how slight the acquaintance had been. The fear came from the realization that if it could happen to Leah, it could happen to any of them. Death. Megan was sure that thought had never occurred to a single one of them. It certainly wasn't something she thought about.

No wonder everyone was shaken to the core.

Dan called out to her just as she was about to leave with her friends. "Go ahead," she told them. "I'll catch up."

Nodding dully, in that same robotic way, the three girls continued to walk slowly towards the car-park.

"I was planning to offer you a lift home," Dan said. His brown eyes were bleak. "But I'm taking Michael back to his house. He's really lost it. I don't think it's a lift you'd want to share. OK if I call you tonight?"

Megan felt no surprise. There was no room inside her at that moment for any emotion other than shock. "Yeah, OK. I'll be home all evening." She wouldn't be going anywhere on this night.

The tension lines around his mouth eased a bit. "Great. Thanks. Talk to you then. Number's in the book?"

It took her a second. "What? Oh, yeah. Adrienne Dunne, Linder Street."

He nodded, waved, and turned to go back to Michael, who was sitting, head in his hands, on a picnic bench between Zoe and David.

Poor Michael, Megan thought, and hoped as she walked towards the car-park that no one in Jade's car would want to talk about Leah's death on the way home. She wasn't ready to talk about it.

No one did.

Megan's mother had already heard about the accident when Megan, drained and shaken, arrived home shortly after seven. Wrapped in a thick bathrobe, her feet bare, Adrienne was sitting on the sofa reading when the front door opened. She tossed the book aside, jumped up and hurried over to Megan. "I just heard about that poor girl. It was on the news. I was so worried about you. Are you all right?"

Megan nodded. "I guess." She sank onto the blue checked sofa. "I mean, it's not like I was hurt or anything. I'm fine. It's just . . . I keep seeing her floating, her yellow jacket all puffed up around her." She shook her head. Her hair, wet and grainy with salt, hung stiffly around her shoulders. "She was already dead when . . . when we got there."

Adrienne sat down beside her daughter.

"It's terrible, sweetie. Maybe Cee was right all along," referring to Jade's mother. "Maybe the lighthouse *should* have been torn down. If it had been, this would never have happened. That girl would still be alive." She looked with concern into her daughter's face.

Adrienne put her arms round Megan then, and let her cry. "It must have been awful. Try not to think about it, darling." Then she said, "You're shivering! You need a nice, hot shower, and I'll make some tea."

Megan lifted her head. There was anguish in her eyes as she asked, "How can I not think about it? She's *dead*! And I was up on that deck just a little while before Leah. The railing could have given way then, instead of later." She pulled away from her mother, sat back against the sofa again, swiping at her eyes with her sleeve. "If that's really what happened."

"If?" Adrienne looked startled. "Is there some question? On the news, they said the railing gave way and she fell."

Megan hadn't meant to let the comment slip out. Her mother had enough on her mind right now, with the prom so close at hand and those three dresses to re-make. Correction, *two* dresses. Oh, God, Leah wouldn't be needing hers now. Still, the last thing in the world Adrienne needed was something more to worry about.

Megan didn't want any more to worry about, either. Her brain was already on overdrive. But she couldn't stop thinking about that Quartet badge. Had it just dropped off a shirt or jumper or blazer earlier, before Leah went anywhere near the lighthouse? The catches on the badges weren't all that trustworthy. Or did the discovery of the badge mean something?

"Sure," Megan said heartily, standing up, "sure, that's what happened. That railing was so old and rickety, it was ready to go at any moment. I had to yell at Dan to stop leaning on it, or he'd have been the one to go flying off the top of the lighthouse instead of Leah."

"Dan?" Adrienne asked with interest.

Megan was relieved to change the subject and talk about Dan. Not that there was that much to tell. But then, after a long drought even a few drops of water were a blessing. Adrienne had been waiting a very long time to hear that her daughter Megan had spent some time with a cute, popular boy. So it probably didn't matter to her that it had been perfectly innocent, that he hadn't asked for a date, or that the two of them hadn't fallen madly, passionately in love. Megan didn't add that he might be calling that night. Because what if he didn't?

Adrienne hung on every word as she put the kettle on for tea.

Megan almost smiled at the obvious effort her mother was making not to overreact. She gets an A for restraint, she thought fondly. No jumping up and down, no hugging her daughter and crying out, "Oh, at last, at last, I knew this day would come!" Adrienne nodded and asked a question here or there and smiled a lot, but she didn't rush to the telephone and order wedding invitations. Possibly because there had been bad news, as well.

"It was just friendly, Mum, that's all," Megan concluded,

accepting the cup of steaming tea her mother handed her. "He's nice. Not full of himself like some of those guys."

"If it hadn't been for that terrible accident, he might have asked to bring you home," Adrienne said, unable this time to hide the excitement in her voice.

She's thinking prom, Megan told herself, suddenly annoyed. "Mum, the only reason he started talking to me was that business at the shop with the dresses. His brother was one of the cops."

Adrienne's expression changed from excited to alarmed. "Oh, heavens, Megan, you didn't talk to him about *that*, did you? I don't want that nasty business spread all over town. I've still got dresses to sell. If that story gets out, they'll be hanging on the rack when the prom is long gone. I'll be stuck with them."

"Dan isn't going to say anything. I promise." Megan was suddenly completely exhausted, as if she'd run all the way from the Point. The long, hot shower her mother had mentioned seemed like a wonderful idea. "Look, thanks for the tea, but I've got to go upstairs. I'm going to have a shower and collapse. Thanks for listening." She managed a wan smile. "It helped, honest."

And it had. She wouldn't have wanted to come home to a dark, quiet house. Not after what had happened. Wouldn't have wanted to go straight to bed with the horrible memory still as fresh and raw as an open, gaping wound. Walking in the front door and finding lights on and her mother there, having someone to talk to, had eased the shock and pain.

Or maybe it was just that she was so grateful. Unlike Leah Markham, she had been allowed to return to her *life*. And had found it waiting for her when she walked in the front door.

She had had her shower and was sitting in bed, a textbook open on her lap although her brain was in no shape to be studying, when Dan called.

They talked for a long time, both careful to avoid the subject of Leah's death. They talked about school, and graduating and what might happen next. They had both been accepted at the same university. Dan planned to go into law, Megan wanted to study graphic design.

But each was painfully aware of the bomb waiting to explode into their conversation.

Finally, Dan sighed and said, "Look, this is silly. Something happened today, we both saw it, and we can't keep tiptoeing around it as if it didn't. Anyway, I think you should know that it definitely wasn't an accident."

Megan's mouth went dry. Her fingers tightened round the receiver. "Not an accident?" she echoed hoarsely.

"No. This is between you and me. Eddie would kill me if he knew I'd said anything before the news was released to the public. That'll be tomorrow morning. So don't tell anyone else, OK? See, she didn't fall right away. They know that now. They figured out that she fell but grabbed onto something with one hand. Part of the railing, maybe. With the other hand, she clawed at the side of the lighthouse. Some of the nail polish from that hand rubbed off on the stone."

The image of Leah dangling so high above the rocks, knowing that if she couldn't pull herself back up to the deck she was going to die, sickened Megan.

"But the knuckles on the first hand," Dan continued heavily, "were bruised and scraped, and the medical examiner found traces of shoe polish in the cuts."

"Shoe polish?"

"Right. *Not* Leah's. She was wearing trainers. This was black shoe polish. As if someone had kicked at her hand until Leah had to let go."

Sour bile rose up into Megan's throat. "Kicked?" she whispered. "Someone kicked her hand away from the only hold she had on that railing?"

"Yeah."

The silence lasted several seconds. "Do they know who it was?" Megan finally managed.

"I guess not." Dan hesitated, then added, "Don't say anything to your mum or Jade, OK? They'll find out in the morning. The whole town will know by then."

"Listen, Megan," Dan said then, "maybe this isn't the right time. I mean, I know it's not. But the prom is only two weeks away if they don't cancel it because of Leah and I don't think they will, so if I'm going to ask this, I have to ask you now. Do you already have a date?"

Megan had waited so long for this moment. Through four long years of high school, she had waited. And now that the moment had actually arrived, she couldn't take it in. The prom? He was asking her to their senior prom? No, that couldn't be right. She must have misunderstood.

"Megan? Did you hear me? Are you already going with someone?"

She struggled to clear her head. She hadn't misunderstood. "No, I . . . no, I don't have a date."

"Oh, great." He sounded relieved. "Like I said today, I hadn't planned to go because I was seriously out of funds. But when I got home tonight there was a graduation cheque from my grandmother waiting for me, so I'm solvent again. Will you go with me?"

Megan thought, I need to say something here. I need to answer him. But her mind had been dealt a dizzying blow and her reaction time had skidded to a standstill. First he had told her that Leah hadn't died accidentally. Now he was asking her to the prom? The two things didn't seem to go together at all.

"Megan, you're making me nervous," Dan's voice said in her ear. "You're taking way too long to answer." His tone was light, but Megan knew he meant it.

She snapped out of it. "I'm sorry. I'm still reeling from what you told me about Leah. I'd love to go to the prom with you. If it isn't cancelled."

"Whew! You had me going there for a minute. Great!" Then he asked, "Have people always called you Megan?"

"Yes. Why?"

"Got any objections to being called Meg?"

"No." The answer came so quickly, she was almost embarrassed.

"Great," he repeated. "Gotta go now. I promised Michael I'd stop over and see how he was doing. But we're all set, right? You're not going to change your mind?"

Megan stared at the phone in her hand. Change her mind? About going to the prom with Dan McGill? She didn't *think* so. "No. That won't happen."

"Let me know what colour your dress is, OK? See you tomorrow."

When Megan had hung up, she knew she should run downstairs, race, *fly*, downstairs to give her mother the good news. Adrienne would be ecstatic.

But her legs weren't ready to move. Because Dan had given her bad news, too, and how was she going to keep that part of the conversation from her mother? Adrienne would be suspicious. She'd want to know what was keeping Megan from jumping around the room and screaming with joy.

And Megan couldn't say that it was the image of Leah Markham dangling by one hand from the observation deck at the lighthouse while someone above her kicked at that ever-weakening hand to make her let go and fall to the rocks and the wild surf below her.

Ten

*I*t's working. No one suspected a thing. I was cool, so cool, acting just like everyone else. Shocked. Grieving. As if I hadn't known a thing about what happened before they knew.

I can keep it up, too, I know I can. All I have to do is concentrate. That's hard, because my head is so full of her scream there's not very much room left for other things, like trying to remember I have to act like everyone else, even though I feel very different now. I'm trying so hard to clear my mind, make that horrible sound go away, but it sticks to my brain as if it's been glued there. With extra-strength Super Glue. Gives me a bad headache.

I already know what I'm going to do if this doesn't work out the way I want it to. If I do have to do it again, it'll be easier the second time. I'm stronger now, smarter. If this stupid headache would just go away, I think I could do anything.

There's a new problem, though. One I hadn't expected.

Megan. She asked too many questions today. Made me nervous. What business is it of hers, anyway? Why doesn't she just butt out? Maybe putting that badge from her shop on the deck was a mistake. I thought it was clever. But she's clever, too, and the discovery of that badge put her brain in gear, I saw that.

Megan could really mess things up. In more ways than one. I saw her talking to a couple of guys at the picnic today, cute guys. And they looked like they were noticing her for the first time. That's not good. I never expected her to be competition. Not her.

Shouldn't I do something about Megan? I really can't afford to take any chances here. She's dangerous. I wouldn't even have to make it look like an accident, because who would connect her to Leah's death? She hardly knew Leah.

Ooh, my head hurts so! I can't even remember right now why I didn't help Leah. Why I let her fall.

Oh, yeah. The prom.

I need to sleep.

I'll do something about Megan tomorrow.

Eleven

The news that Leah Markham had died under "suspicious circumstances" was released to the public early the following morning.

In spite of that bombshell, classes at Glenview High were held as scheduled, although it was announced that there would be no school on the following day, Friday, to allow the victim's classmates to attend her funeral. No one, not even the rowdiest students who hadn't given Leah's fate a second thought, shouted "Hooray!" at the announcement.

A sombre, fearful silence had fallen over the entire school. Leah's closest friends trailed through the hallways with pale, sometimes tear-streaked faces. Beth, Leah's best friend, had chosen to stay at home, as had Michael.

There were, of course, those students who were not quite as shattered.

At lunch, Megan had expected to talk about the terrible

event of the day before, especially now that the whole town knew Leah's death hadn't been accidental.

Instead, they'd only been sitting in the unusually quiet, yellow-walled canteen for a few minutes when Lucy asked eagerly, "So, who do you think Michael will take to the prom now?"

Megan gasped. Her sandwich, halfway to her mouth, came to an abrupt halt in mid-air. "*What* did you say?"

Lucy didn't flinch. "I *said*, who do we think Michael will ask to the prom now? I mean, he's not going to miss his own prom, right? Might even be king this year, if he asks the right girl."

"I'm sure he'll get it. He'd make a great king." Jade agreed. She had tried another new hairstyle, but by mid morning it was already coming undone, a bird's nest caught in a hurricane. She had tried to repair the damage. Two girls at a table behind them were pointing at Jade, and whispering and giggling. Unaware, Jade continued, "Who *is* going to be queen this year? Not that I care, of course, since I probably won't be there. But everyone seemed to think that Leah was a sure thing. Who else is there?"

"Beth hasn't been queen yet," Sophie said. "And I like her the best of the Pops."

"Never mind the queen," Lucy said irritably. "It's the kings we should be interested in. I personally think that Michael

Danz is much cuter than Jordan Nelson. Besides, Michael is available now and Jordan isn't. He's Beth's date." She grinned. "Michael smiled at me at the picnic, during the softball game. When Leah wasn't around, of course," she added hastily.

Megan had been stricken speechless by Lucy's callousness. Now, she found her voice. It slid from her mouth quietly, but it was laced with pure acid. "Lucy, has Michael Danz ever once in his life said hello to you? Has he ever given a single sign that he is even aware of your existence on this planet?" She knew it was cruel. But Megan felt no remorse. How could Lucy be so clueless? How insensitive did you have to be to drool over a boy whose girlfriend had been dead less than twenty-four hours?

Insensitive enough, apparently, not to be wounded by Megan's unkind questions. Lucy didn't even redden. "Just that smile yesterday. But there's always hope. And I'm not the only one who's thinking this way, Megan. No one at this table has a date for her own senior prom. We all know that the pretty, popular girls already have dates, so Michael isn't going to have a lot to choose from. And if there is anyone at this table *not* hoping he'll choose her, speak now or forever hold your peace."

"I'm not," Megan said, keeping her eyes on her sandwich. This didn't seem like the best moment in the world to tell them she was going, but she didn't want them finding out from someone else. "Dan McGill asked me last night."

All three faces went blank. Jade stared at Megan. "Asked you what?"

"Asked me to the prom." Megan was grateful that people around them had begun talking. The buzz of conversation, though it was quieter than usual, might keep everyone in the room from overhearing her friends' reaction to what she had just told them.

"*The* Dan McGill?" Lucy repeated. "Asked *you* to go to the prom with him?"

Annoyed, Megan said with some heat, "Stranger things *have* happened, Lucy. Don't make it sound like this news ranks right up there with someone giving birth to an alien's baby."

Sophie shook a headful of frizzy red curls and breathed a "Wow!" that spoke volumes. "I thought he was taking Zoe. Everyone thought so." She shifted her thin frame on the metal folding chair. "Well, no wonder you're not interested in who Michael might invite now."

Jade said nothing, but her eyes suddenly looked suspiciously bright.

Megan knew how Jade must be feeling. They had spent every prom night throughout high school together, having what they called a "non-prom party." Freshman year, they hadn't expected to be invited. In their sophomore year, they'd held only a slight hope that some cute junior or senior might notice they were alive. It hadn't happened. Junior year, they'd been much more optimistic, since by that time they actually knew more guys. But those guys had asked other girls, not them.

Sometimes their non-prom party had been held at Jade's house, sometimes at Megan's. They'd held it on the Point once. That had been fun, but only Megan was willing to climb up to the top of the lighthouse. So she'd had to go up alone in the dark. That *had* been a bit creepy. Still, they'd always had fun, and they had already planned a get-together at Jade's house this year. Megan's announcement meant that things would be different. There would be only Jade, Sophie, and Lucy at their non-prom festivities. Megan knew that had to hurt Jade.

"Your mother must be jumping for joy," Jade said then, toying with her hair. "Has she already sold the blue dress?"

"No. She was saving it for me. Hid it upstairs in the Sweatbox." Megan didn't add that Adrienne was also saving the turquoise for Jade, just in case. She could ask Joseph, she told herself in an effort to ease the pain she felt for Jade. She *could*.

Not one of them had said it was wonderful that she was going to the prom.

"I wonder why he's not going with Zoe," Lucy said lazily.

"She asked someone from her brother's college." Megan pushed her sandwich aside.

"Dan must have been really upset," Jade said, shoving her own uneaten sandwich to the side. "Everyone just assumed Zoe was going with him."

Irritated by the implication that she was second choice, Megan said, "He hadn't planned on going at all." She had no intention of agreeing that she was Dan's consolation prize because Zoe Buffet had chosen someone else. "No money. But his grandmother sent him a cheque."

"Never mind Dan McGill," Lucy said impatiently. "We all thought he was already taken, anyway. It's Michael we need to concentrate on."

Megan shook her head in disbelief. They had not said one word about the news release from the police department that morning. "I can't believe we're even discussing the prom. You don't find it utterly terrifying," she asked quietly, "that Leah's death wasn't an accident? That someone *kicked* her hand away from that railing?"

Lucy looked up in surprise. "What's that got to do with us? Leah's a Pop. We're not. Whoever had it in for her probably doesn't even know we exist." A dreamy look appeared in her eyes. "I wonder," she mused out loud, "if your mother still has that gorgeous pale pink dress, the one with the long, full skirt."

"You're too short for a dress like that." Sophie thought for a minute, then added with hope in her voice, "Michael's in my maths class. I've helped him solve more than one really horrendous problem. I wonder if he remembers."

Annoyed that they weren't happier for her and repulsed by the talk about Michael Danz, Megan stood up. "I can't deal with this." She picked up her books. "Well, don't lose hope, any of you," she added sarcastically. "There's always a chance that at the *funeral* tomorrow, maybe right in the middle of the service, Michael will walk up to one of you and invite you to the prom. Just in case, you might want to run over to Quartet after school today and grab yourself a dress. Mum has a few left. Just don't tell her who you hope to be going with, or she'll be as repulsed as I am."

"Easy for you to talk," Sophie retorted. "You already *have* a date. Which you can thank Zoe for, if you ask me."

"I *didn't* ask you." Megan turned to leave.

"Besides, Megan," Jade said quietly, "it's not like Michael was always faithful to Leah. Everyone knows he fooled around sometimes. So maybe he's not as shattered as you think he should be."

"I'm outta here," Megan snapped. Five seconds later, she was striding down the main hallway, her cheeks high with colour. She was angry that her very best friends for years now, hadn't shared her happiness at being invited to the prom. And she couldn't believe they were all, even Jade, hoping to be invited themselves by someone whose girlfriend of several years had just been killed. Revolting.

Later, as she and Jade worked together at Quartet, there was an uneasy, strained silence between them. During a lull in customer activity, Megan went up to the Sweatbox to iron fabric, putting on a CD for company.

Jade followed her. She stood in the doorway, cracking her knuckles nervously. Megan ignored her, concentrating instead on keeping the wobbly old board steady on its wooden legs.

"You don't think someone like Michael Danz would ever ask someone like me out, do you?" Jade finally asked, her voice low.

Megan reached over to turn off the CD. She put the iron down. "Jade, Leah was *killed* yesterday! No one's talking about that. You all sat there at lunch and talked about who Michael might take to the prom now. He probably won't even *go*! Aren't you the least bit worried about what happened to Leah up on that deck?"

Jade walked over to stand at the long, narrow, open window. Late-day shadows from outside highlighted the sharp angles in her face. "I didn't *like* Leah, Megan. That's no surprise. None of us did. Just because she was a big deal at school doesn't mean she was nice. She wasn't. Do you think if I'd been killed, Leah would have stayed home from the prom?"

She had a point. "No. But Jade, aren't you *worried* about *who* killed her? I mean, someone deliberately kicked her hand away from the post. Maybe pushed her over the edge, too. Doesn't that scare you?"

Jade picked up a bolt of red fabric, began smoothing its folds. "Like Lucy said, Megan, what does that have to do with us? Leah was a Pop. Maybe she made one of her many friends angry. We don't run with that crowd. So what do we have to worry about?" She laid the bolt of fabric back on its shelf. "Maybe it was a passer-by who killed her. Either way, if we stay away from the Point and," her voice hardened, "we don't suddenly become wildly popular, we're OK, right? In fact," her voice slowed as a new thought formed, "now that I think about it, maybe we wallflowers are better off. Leah was going to the prom, am I right? But now she's not."

Megan's eyes narrowed. "What's that supposed to mean?"

Jade shrugged. "First the dresses were ruined, and then Leah, who was a cert for queen, flies off the deck of the lighthouse and becomes fish food."

"Jade!"

"Sorry. But don't you see a connection here, Megan? You're a very smart person. I can't believe you haven't already seen the link between those two very nasty events. It's the prom, Megan. Anyone can see that." Then, as she walked back to the door to go downstairs, she added, "Look, I'm sorry I was such an idiot at lunch. I really am glad Dan asked you to the prom. At least I would be, if all this hadn't happened. I don't know, Megan, maybe you'd be better off celebrating with us. You don't want to end up like Leah. Or like one of those three prom dresses, right?"

Fighting desperately to stay calm, Megan put the music on again and resumed her ironing. "I'm not going to end up under someone's tyres, Jade. Don't worry about it." I'll do enough worrying for both of us, she thought but didn't say. "And maybe I would have acted the same way if you'd been asked to the prom instead of me."

"No, you wouldn't have." Jade went back downstairs.

Adrienne came up a few minutes later. She looked puzzled. "Sweetheart, have you seen Leah's red dress?"

Megan looked up from the ironing board, a mixture of surprise and distaste on her face. "Mum! Have you forgotten she's not going to be needing it now?"

"No, of course I haven't. And I would never put it back on display. I thought I'd donate it to the theatre department at school. Someone should get some use out of it." Frowning,

Adrienne stood in the middle of the cramped space, hands on her slim hips. "But I can't find it."

"Where was it?"

"Hanging in a plastic bag behind the register. I called her on Monday and told her it was ready. She was going to pick it up early this morning. But of course. . ." Adrienne's voice trailed off.

Megan switched off the iron. "I'll help you look."

But, though they covered every inch of space in the entire shop, enlisting Jade's and Joseph's help, there was no sign of Leah's red dress.

"I don't understand this at all," Adrienne said when they finally gave up.

Neither did Megan. But the dress was gone.

Dan called that night, and he and Megan talked for over an hour. Although she was curious about the police investigation into Leah's death, she didn't ask him about it. She didn't want him to think she was using him for information. And she didn't tell him about the missing prom dress, either. Too weird.

Jade already knew about the missing dress, but they didn't talk about it when she called later, except when she said, "I told Sophie and Lucy. They thought it was pretty freakish. I still think someone from her family came in and got it.

Maybe we were all busy somewhere else and they were too upset to talk about it, so they just took the dress and left. The bag had a tag with Leah's name right there on the front, and it was already paid for, right?"

Right. But Megan found that scenario difficult to believe. Hard to imagine a member from that devastated family coming into the shop to pick up a prom dress that Leah wouldn't ever wear.

Sophie and Lucy were right. The disappearance of the dress *was* freakish. But it paled in comparison to Leah's death.

What it *did* do, though, was fortify Jade's theory that the prom was somehow involved in these recent ugly events. Weird that Jade herself hadn't mentioned that just now, hadn't pushed the theft at Megan as additional proof that she was right. Jade *did* so like to be right.

It rained all day Friday, a light but steady, chilly shower that turned the grass spongy at the cemetery. Standing under a canopy at the graveyard following the service, Megan wished fiercely that the sun were shining, that the air was dry and warm. Leah had died in cold wetness. She shouldn't have to be buried in it, too.

When it was all over, Megan was standing in line to pay her respects to the Markham family when she overheard Leah's older sister Rebecca say sadly, "No, the police have no idea. It's so hard for us to believe that anyone would harm our Leah. She was so popular. Everyone loved her."

Not quite everyone, Megan thought. But her heart went out to Leah's family.

The image of Leah dangling above the rocks, terrified, knowing she was about to die, made Megan so ill, she had to break from the line. She rushed across the sodden ground to find shelter on a wooden bench under a large tree. Slipping free of uncomfortable shoes, she tucked her legs up underneath her to keep her stockinged feet off the wet ground, and watched the line of mourners greet the family.

When her stomach finally quieted, she decided to return to the line.

But when she saw Michael, wearing a dark suit, surrounded by a cluster of girls, Megan's stomach revolted. Some of the girls were crying, among them Sophie, Lucy and Jade. Were they all really expressing sympathy? None of them had known Leah well, if at all. Zoe and Lily were in the cluster, too, and Beth, hanging on to Jordan's arm, as if for support. Zoe looked completely stunned, Lily and Beth devastated. They were crying.

At least, Megan thought in disgust, those three were Leah's best mates, which is more than I can say for *my* friends. How obvious can you get? It's sickening.

"Bad day for a funeral, right?" Dan's voice said in Megan's ear.

She jumped, startled. "Oh. I guess. Is there such a thing as a good day for a funeral?"

"Good point. New shoes?" he asked, pointing to her feet. "Too small?"

"No. Too big. I was in a hurry when I bought them." The constant slipping up and down on her heels bothered her. She slid the shoes back on, wishing she'd worn more comfortable ones.

Dan's dark hair was wet, curling along his forehead and over his ears. "You haven't had any more trouble at Quartet, have you?"

The question surprised Megan. She stood up. "No ... Why?"

"Well, I don't want to scare you," he said quietly, "but the cops think there might be a connection between what happened at your shop and Leah's death."

"The connection isn't the shop," Megan said quietly. "It's the prom."

"What?"

"It's the prom. Has to be." She looked up at him. "Prom dresses ruined, Leah a sure thing for queen ... what else could it be?"

"The prom?" He thought about that for a minute. "Any idea why?"

"Nope. Not me. Haven't a clue. Do you?"

He shook his head. "Someone who isn't going, I suppose. Upset that they're not going."

"Upset enough to *kill*? Over a *dance*?"

"It sounds crazy, I know. But Meg," his eyes on hers, "kicking Leah's hand away from that railing was an act of insanity, wasn't it? Bad enough that the person up there with her didn't help her, and didn't get help for her after she'd fallen. Now we know they actually *made* her fall. You're right, a normal person would never think about killing because of a prom, no matter how many people in the canteen say, 'I'd kill to go to the prom'. They don't mean it, not literally. But a sick, twisted mind might think it was necessary. Might even think it was perfectly OK. Who knows?"

When Megan said nothing, he added hastily, "Look, I shouldn't have brought it up. It's a grim enough day without talking about this now. I'm sorry. I didn't mean to scare you."

Megan knew he wanted her to say, "Oh, that's OK. I'm not scared at all."

But she couldn't say that. Because it would have been a lie.

Twelve

The crowd was beginning to disperse. People were anxious to get away from the sadness of the burial site and out of the nasty weather.

"Do the police have any idea who did it?" Megan asked Dan. "Who kicked Leah's foot off that deck?"

"No. Eddie says they don't. Walkers hang around the Point sometimes. But even if they knew for sure who it was, Eddie'd never tell me, not until an arrest was made. He shouldn't have told me as much as he did. He was tired when he got home after it happened, and needed to talk, and I was there, so. . ."

Like me and Mum the other night, Megan thought. Sometimes you just couldn't keep things, especially bad things, inside. And maybe you shouldn't. Might make your brain explode or something.

"Want a lift home?" Dan asked. "I've got my car."

"Jade brought me. But I'm not going home. I have to go straight to the shop."

"I can take you there. Would Jade mind? I mean, if you want to."

If she wanted to? Did she want world peace? An end to starvation? Did she want the person who had shoved Leah off that deck safely behind bars? "That'd be nice. Thanks. Let me go and tell her. Wait here." She didn't want Dan witnessing Jade's reaction. It probably wouldn't be pretty.

To Megan's astonishment, Jade didn't seem to mind at all. "Oh, that's OK," she told a stupefied Megan. "We're not going home, anyway." She waved a hand to include Sophie and Lucy. They were already on their way over to Michael, who was surrounded by his own friends. Zoe still looked as if she were in shock, her eyes blank, her face drawn. Beth and Lily had stopped crying, but seemed drained, their usual vitality gone. "We're all going back to Leah's house to pay our respects," Jade said.

Megan raised an eyebrow. "All? Meaning. . . ?"

"Oh, you know. Sophie and Lucy and I, and all of Michael's other friends."

"Michael's *other* friends?" Jade barely knew Michael Danz. None of us know him, Megan thought, any more than we knew Leah. Sophie had been on Leah's basketball team at school but Megan doubted that they'd ever exchanged more than two words. Not one of them could stand her, and they'd never made any secret of that. "You're going back to her house?"

"Yep." Jade's eyes were still on Michael.

Megan couldn't stand it. "Happy hunting," she said caustically and left to return to Dan.

The disgust must have been apparent in her face, because he asked, "Problems? Is she cross with you?"

"What? Oh, no, she's not cross. They have plans."

"Would you rather go with them?"

"Absolutely not. But aren't you expected at Leah's house?"

He took her hand as they walked through the rain along the cemetery road to the car-park. "That place is going to be mobbed. Leah knows . . . knew I'm not good in crowded places. She wouldn't expect me to show up there."

She wouldn't have expected Jade to show up, either, Megan thought, wiping her face dry with a tissue when she was sitting in Dan's new red Mini. Or Lucy or Sophie.

Could they really be that desperate to go to their senior prom?

And had any of them been wearing black shoes at the picnic?

That thought was so involuntary and so stunning it took Megan's breath away. She reeled with the shock of it. She couldn't really have wondered that, could she? What was wrong with her? Sophie might not be the brightest person in the world and Lucy was bossy and cynical. But they'd been Megan's friends for years, and Megan had never seen either of them commit a deliberate act of cruelty. As for Jade, she couldn't even bear to shoo away the alley cats when Adrienne told her to.

Whatever had happened at the top of the lighthouse, it couldn't possibly have anything to do with her friends. No way.

Besides, this wasn't one of those disgusting teen horror films where the girl was so desperate for a date, she took a chain-saw to anyone who stood in her way. This was real life. As in, Leah was really dead.

As Dan turned the ignition key, he asked lightly, "You haven't changed your mind about the prom, have you? I mean, if you're worried about a connection between it and Leah's death. Lily tells me they're not going to cancel. She checked with Trotter." Trotter was Glenview High's vice principal. "He said cancelling would just make things worse. I think he's right."

"I haven't changed my mind." Megan shook raindrops from her hair. "And my dress is blue. Deep blue."

"Unlike shallow blue," Dan said seriously as they left the cemetery road for the main road.

Megan laughed. "But don't hire a limo, OK? Too pretentious. Can't we just go in this?"

110

"A Mini? You want to arrive at your senior prom in a Mini?" He glanced sideways at her. "Hey, look, the cheque from my grandmother had more than one zero. I can deal with a limo."

"No, I mean it. I'd really rather go in this."

"Finally," he said with a grin, "what I've been looking for all my life. A cheap date."

Megan laughed again, but then wondered if she'd said the wrong thing. Zoe would never have settled for anything less than a limo, and Zoe was the kind of person Dan was used to. Maybe, Megan thought, my inexperience at attending proms is showing.

Too bad. She really *did* think limos were a waste of money, so why should she pretend otherwise? If he wanted Zoe, he'd have asked Zoe.

But he probably *did*, Megan. Lucy's voice. What was it doing inside Megan's head? He probably did ask Zoe, Lucy's voice continued matter-of-factly, only Zoe said no because she wanted to go with a college guy. And all of the other Pops were already taken. So Dan settled for you. But of course you already knew that, right? Everyone at school does.

Shut up, Lucy! Megan ordered. Dan did *not* ask Zoe. He was broke. He said so, and I believe him. It's not his fault everyone at school assumes he wanted to take her.

111

Lucy's voice subsided. But her words continued to ring in Megan's head.

I don't care, she decided finally. I don't care *why* he asked me. I'm going with him, and that's all that counts.

"The cops are going to question Michael," Dan said suddenly. "Because he admitted they'd had an argument on the day of the picnic."

It took Megan a few seconds to make the switch from Lucy's snide, imagined comments to Leah's brutal death. When she had, she said, "They argued a lot. But they always made up." She glanced over at Dan. "They can't think he did it!"

He shrugged. "Why not? Eddie says you always look to the closest person . . . a husband, a boyfriend, a sibling. . ."

"But Michael loved Leah!" Megan remembered then Jade's quiet comment in the canteen about Michael being unfaithful to his girlfriend. Was that true? With whom? Whoever she was, maybe the police should talk to her, find out if she now expected Michael to take her to the prom, with Leah out of the way. Wouldn't she be someone who would have a reason not to help Leah back up onto the observation deck?

Gross!

If the police hauled Michael downtown for questioning today, he wouldn't be at the Markham house when Jade and the others arrived. They'd be crushed. No matter what they

112

said about paying their respects, the unpleasant truth was that Michael Danz, who no longer had a prom date, was their only reason for going over there.

When they parked in front of Quartet, Dan turned to her and said, "I want you to know something. You're the first and only girl I've asked to the prom. I just thought you had a right to know that."

As if he'd read her mind. Megan rejoiced. Take that, Lucy Dowd! "Thanks for telling me, Dan." She grinned. "And you're the first guy I said yes to." No need to add that he was the first person who'd asked. He probably already knew that, but he was too nice to point it out.

Then she stopped grinning because he was kissing her and she didn't want him to bump into her teeth.

Before she got out of the car, he said, "Decorating committee meeting tomorrow afternoon. I know you're on it. See you there."

Megan frowned. "You're not on the committee." She'd already been to three meetings.

He grinned. "I am now."

Megan was smiling as she walked into the shop. When she'd gone to the first meeting, with Jade and the others, Zoe had looked surprised to see them there. Later, she had asked Megan sympathetically, "Isn't it hard to decorate when you're not going to the prom?"

Megan had replied, "I'm never going to be a patient in paediatrics at the hospital, either, Zoe, but I still decorate there at Christmas."

There weren't that many customers in the shop, but her mother was glad to see her. She asked about the funeral, and then said briskly, "Well, if you'll handle things down here, I'll just go on up to the Sweatbox and work on those dresses." She frowned. "I still haven't found the red one, though. I can't imagine what happened to it."

Those dresses. Megan had almost forgotten. Was there really a connection between the destruction of those prom dresses and the terrible thing that had happened to Leah? How could there be? And what had become of Leah's dress?

She pushed the ugly, frightening thoughts out of her mind. Thinking stuff like that would ruin her mood. Maybe Dan would call later and offer her a lift home after work. It was Friday, which meant they were open until nine. If her mother had a date with Sam Hollister, the lawyer she'd been seeing, Sam would pick her up at the shop. Megan wasn't sure why, but for the first time, she was uneasy about going home alone to an empty house. She didn't like the feeling.

The rest of the day went by quickly. Megan received two phone calls just before closing time. One was from Dan, telling her he was with Michael at Leah's house now that the crowd had gone, and he didn't think he'd be leaving until ten. Would she wait for him at the shop? He'd take her home.

"Sure. I'll do some studying, clean up round here a bit." Then she asked if her friends were still there. He said no, they'd left a long time ago.

Megan was a little disappointed that they hadn't come to the shop. It had been crowded later this afternoon. A lot of people had stopped in after the funeral, maybe thinking that buying a new shirt or skirt would lift their spirits. She could have done with Jade's help. But maybe it was just as well. She wanted to talk about the prom, and she probably shouldn't do that around her friends.

The second call was from Joseph. Adrienne had let him go home early when he'd finished his errands. He sounded angry. "You made Jade cry."

Confused, Megan asked him what he was talking about.

"She's been crying. I saw her this afternoon, after the funeral, and her eyes were all swollen. I knew it wasn't because of Leah, because why would that make Jade cry? She didn't even like Leah. So I asked her, and she said it was because you're going to the prom and she isn't."

Megan didn't know what to say.

"I can't believe you're going with McGill," Joseph continued angrily. "He's one of *them*, Megan. The ones we

115

always made fun of, you and me and Jade. It's like you're going over to the other side or something."

"That's ridiculous, Joseph!" Megan couldn't believe what she was hearing. What difference did it make to Joseph *who* she dated? It was Jade he was crazy about, not her. "Dan is a nice guy. Anyway, it's really none of your business. I'm sorry about Jade, but she could be going, too, if she really wanted to." She didn't add that Jade wasn't going because she, too, wanted to be going with someone like Dan.

The conversation left Megan very uncomfortable. Was Joseph right? Hadn't she meant all those cracks she'd made about the Pops? Had she just been pretending, wanting to be a part of their group all along? Was she a hypocrite, as Joseph had implied?

When she opened the back door to sweep around outside before leaving, a mangy old black alley cat was waiting expectantly. "Oh, all right," Megan said, knowing her mother would have a fit if she knew. "I was going to have a glass of milk and a sandwich before I left. I guess I can share a drop or two of the milk with you. But that's all you're getting."

The milk carton in the small fridge was almost empty. Deciding on Coke for herself instead, she poured the white liquid into a saucer and put it outside for the cat. Then she finished tidying up, totalled up the cash, did the hoovering, made herself a sandwich and took it upstairs to the Sweatbox, where she climbed through the window to sit on the fire escape and eat.

Friday night. The car-park across the alley, in front of Impeccable Tastes, was full. Her mother and Sam were probably inside, enjoying prime steak or salmon.

Maybe, Megan thought, biting into her tuna sandwich, since we're not renting a limo for the prom, we can afford to have dinner there. That would be nice. Romantic.

When she had finished eating, she went back downstairs, tossed the empty milk carton, sandwich crusts, and paper plate into the rubbish and bundled it up, slinging the black plastic bag over her shoulder to take it to the big bin in the alley. Turning off the lights, she opened the door, stepped outside, slammed the door tightly behind her, and turned to double-check the lock. It was almost ten. She'd wait for Dan in front of the shop.

As she turned round, the toe of her shoe hit something on the ground.

Megan glanced down, thinking she had bumped into the saucer that she'd forgotten was there. Good thing she'd remembered, or Adrienne would have seen it sitting there first thing in the morning. She would not have been happy.

But it wasn't the saucer Megan's toe had hit, it was the cat. It was lying very, very still, its whiskered face contorted in agony, frozen that way forever, its eyes bulging, its legs extended stiffly.

Megan stared down at it, knowing without even checking that the animal was lying very, very still because, it was very, very dead.

Thirteen

The alley was dark and quiet. Only muted sounds of music and conversation came from inside Impeccable Tastes, its double glass doors standing open to the balmy evening breeze. Megan glanced round, hoping to find someone who could come and help, but there was no one.

She looked down at the cat again. Dead? It was dead? But just a little while ago, it had mewed gratefully when she slid the saucer of milk in front of it.

She dropped the rubbish bag and crouched beside the stiff, black carcass. The cat was old, with grey around its whiskers, and very skinny. She couldn't help wishing that it had ended its life elsewhere. She couldn't leave it where it was. Adrienne might not be fond of the alley cats, but she was a pet lover in general, and she'd be very upset if this was the first thing she came across when she opened the shop in the morning.

Megan loathed the idea of putting the cat into the bin, but she didn't see that she had a choice. It's dead, Megan, she told herself firmly, it doesn't care where you put it. She could wait until Dan came, ask him to do it. But she was the one who had fed it, and in some strange way, that made her feel responsible for it.

A thought tugged at Megan's brain, like the cat scratching earlier at the back door. If it had died because it was old, why was its face so horribly distorted, its teeth showing in a grimace of what looked like anguish?

She got up, unlocked the door, went back inside to grab a section of newspaper waiting to be recycled. When she had locked the door again, she knelt down beside the cat. Gingerly, carefully, she rolled it onto the newspaper and quickly thrust it into the black plastic bag. At the last minute, she dumped the saucer in, too. Wouldn't be using *that* again. Then she quickly twisted the neck of the bag shut and re-tied the twist tie. Ugh! Her hands shook. Creepy.

Hoisting the bag again, she hurried to the huge bin. Its giant green metal lid was already open.

Megan heaved the bag over the edge of the bin, her mind on the cat inside. She felt sorry for it. It couldn't have had a very nice life, and an alley was no place to die.

There was a sound behind her. Megan would have turned, had she had time. But she didn't. Because in the next second, cold hands reached out to grab her legs and lift her up. . . .

Megan cried out. Her hands flew out to clutch at the front of the bin. But the grip around her lower body was stronger than her own. Angry. It felt angry, that grip on her legs, squeezing the flesh painfully as it lifted her lower body higher, higher.

"Stop it!" Megan cried, feeling her hands on the bin being tugged away. "What are you *doing*? Stop!"

Her heart was pounding so with terror, she could feel her ribs shaking. At the very last second, her brain kicked into gear and Megan kicked off one loose black shoe. If she couldn't stop herself from being thrown into the disgusting bin, she would at least leave a sign behind that she was in there. Losing the shoe was the only thing she could think of to do. She could only hope her captor hadn't heard the shoe fall.

He must not have, because the cruel hands didn't release their grip to scoop up the discarded shoe. Instead, they gave Megan's body one forceful, cruel shove that sent her flying up and over the edge of the bin. Her hands were ripped away from the rim and she fell into the dark, smelly interior.

She landed in a sea of plastic bags. They made a squooshing sound when she smacked into them on her stomach and sank slightly into their folds. Unhurt, but dazed, she lay there for a second or two, surrounded by darkness and fetid smells and the closeness of a day's heat stored within a metal enclosure.

Before she could clear her head enough to pull herself upright, there was an ominous creaking sound above her.

Megan lifted her head to see the starlit sky disappearing.

"No!" she screamed desperately. "No, don't *do* that!"

The lid slammed down upon her, erasing the last little bit of air and light.

Fourteen

Megan had never been in such complete, utter darkness. Dark as an underground cave . . . a coffin . . . a grave. The only light at all came from a small hole in one corner at the bottom of the bin.

The bin was only half full, allowing Megan some headroom. With the lid closed, the smell was terrible. Most of the rubbish was enclosed in bags, but not all. Her foot slid against what she was sure had to be a banana skin, rotted from the heat, and her left hand encountered a mass of something so soft and mushy, she didn't want to think about what it might be.

A rustling sound off to her left froze her where she lay sprawled across piles of slippery, lumpy plastic. Something dark and furry scooted across the top of the heap, brushing against Megan's arm as it passed. She flew upright. The dark, furry thing squeezed out of the hole in the base and disappeared.

Megan shuddered violently. A squirrel, she told herself desperately, or maybe a cat. Not a rat, it wasn't a rat.

It . . . was . . . not . . . a . . . rat, she insisted silently. And it's gone, it's gone!

She'd heard a lock snapping on the lid after it fell. But locked or not, there was no way she could lift that heavy lid by herself.

And I am, she thought, panic rising within her, by myself. Very much by myself in this dark, putrid, airless place. Trapped.

Panicking, she crawled, slipping and sliding, along the top of the heap until she was close enough to one side of the bin to bang on it with her fists. She banged and pounded and shouted at the top of her lungs and when that didn't work and no one came to get her out and her hands were bruised and bleeding, she thrust out her legs and began kicking with all her might.

Nothing. No one shouted in answer to her shouts, and no one came to save her.

What good would the shoe she had left behind do if there was no one out there to see it?

Megan sank back on her heels, breathing hard, her throat sore from shouting. "I want to get *out* of here!" she cried hoarsely. Tears of anger and fear squeezed their way down her cheeks. "Someone let me out of here, *please*!"

Someone would come along. Someone *would*. The restaurant was right there, right behind her. People would be leaving. She would hear them talking or laughing and she would scream and shout and bang on the walls of the bin and someone would hear her and come and let her out. Out, out, out, she wanted to get *out*!

How had this happened? The cat had died, she had wrapped it in newspaper, brought it to the bin. . .

And someone had thrown her in here.

Why?

A joke? Was this supposed to be funny?

No. Megan knew, as surely as she knew that if someone didn't release her soon she was really going to totally lose it, that this had not been meant as a joke. Couldn't have been.

Such an awful thing to do to someone, this . . . this horrible thing that had been done to her, shutting her up in such a smelly, hot place, dark, dark, so dark . . . noises, there were noises again but not outside, where they could do her some good, inside, here, with *her*, noises where there shouldn't be any. Another rat? Please, not another rat!

Eyes wide with terror, Megan turned her head towards where the sound was coming from. The little hole at the bottom of the bin.

There was a flash of light from outside the hole. Megan, crouched on the plastic bags, her breath coming in small, anxious gasps, kept her eyes fastened on that one spot. The light came closer, closer. Something was being pushed in through the hole. Something orange, red, yellow, lighting the end of a long, white cylinder.

The cylinder was a rolled-up newspaper. Someone outside the bin was inserting a rolled-up newspaper into the hole.

And the orange, red, and yellow was there because the newspaper was on fire.

Megan's heart jumped into her throat. Fire! Someone was setting fire to this place where she was imprisoned? If the fire caught, the bin would fill with foul smoke in seconds. She would suffocate. She would die a horrible, choking death.

Skidding and sliding, ducking down to avoid cracking the top of her head on the lid, Megan moved as swiftly as she could across the top of the heap until she reached the corner, intending to stamp out the fire with her remaining shoe.

Too late. The edge of a bundle of newspapers someone had been too thoughtless to recycle, had already caught. Yellow flames gobbled it up hungrily. Megan was still wearing the skirt she'd worn to the funeral. Heat from the fire seared her legs, protected only by her tights, which were no protection at all.

Still crouching low, she backed away. As she did so, she reached out to snatch up the first sack of plastic her hands touched. It was full, and very heavy. She had to turn and use both arms to lift it and heave it down on top of the blazing newspaper bundle.

"Meg?" a voice called from outside. Dan's voice. No one else called her Meg. But it sounded far away. Where was he? Over by the shop?

Instead of smothering the fire, as Megan had hoped it would, the plastic bag became engulfed in flame. Hot, hungry fingers reached up and caught a strand of Megan's hair, hanging loose around her face. She slapped out the flame and began hastily backing away again. In her haste, she forgot about the heavy metal lid, and the top of her head slammed into it with a sharp, cracking sound, sending her to her knees. The pain was unbearable. Her left knee landed on something metal, sharp-edged as a razor. Megan felt the skin there split open, felt the blood spilling out. She put one hand to the top of her head, felt it warm and sticky there, too.

"Meg? Are you here?" It was Dan. Across the alley at the shop, probably wondering why he hadn't found her waiting there for him, as she'd promised.

The smoke and heat were stifling. In just minutes, all four metal sides would be too hot for her to touch, let alone pound on to summon help.

"I'm here," Megan croaked. Her eyes were watering, and her chest hurt. "I'm in here, Dan."

She knew even as she said it that he wasn't close enough to hear her kittenish-weak voice. He had to still be at the shop. On the other side of the car-park. Would he see the smoke, run to the bin, bringing him close enough so that she wouldn't need to shout?

"Meg?" Pounding on the alley door at Quartet. "Meg? It's Dan! Have you fallen asleep in there?"

Wrong door, Megan thought, trying to dredge up enough strength to crawl away from the flames. You're pounding on the wrong door, Dan. A spasm of coughing seized her. She couldn't get any air.

Damn, Megan thought as, still coughing and choking, her body sank into the sea of plastic and her tear-filled eyes closed. Damn. I was going to go to the prom.

Maybe that's why I'm in here, was her last, stunning thought as she slid into unconsciousness.

Fifteen

*C*rude. A bin? Very crude. Amateurish. Should have come up with something smoother.

Actually, I meant to plan something clever. As hard as it is to think these days, with Leah screaming in my head all the time, I knew I could come up with something. But I hadn't yet.

And then I had such a bad day. Suddenly, there wasn't any more time left. So I had to substitute acts that weren't clever at all. I had no choice.

First, I learned that Michael has no intention of going to the prom. With anyone. Out of respect for Leah, her family announced. Respect, eh? Out of guilt is more like it. He never told Leah about us, the way he should have, and he doesn't know that I enlightened her just before she died. So why would he beat himself up about it? As far as he knows, she was completely ignorant of what was going on, and don't they say that ignorance is bliss? So why can't he tell himself that she died blissfully unaware of his treachery? And take me to the prom, the way he promised he would all along.

I was a fool. He never intended to take me. I could have asked someone else, and none of this would be happening. But Michael kept saying he was going to tell Leah the truth and break his prom date with her. Then he kept putting it off, saying he knew it would upset her and he had to pick exactly the right time and place. Which he promised he would do.

He lied.

So I finally picked the time and place myself, and told her what was going on. Only then it didn't matter because she died and we'll never know if it upset her or not, will we?

I wasted all that time on him for nothing.

Finding that out was bad enough. But then I figured, I'd just ask someone else. Someone almost as good as Michael Danz. Dan.

That was when the real blow came. That was when I learned something that set my brain on fire.

Dan plans to take Megan to the prom!

I can't believe it. Megan?

I know this because the minute Leah's mother announced that Michael was going away for the summer to "recover from our darling daughter's tragic death", I walked right over to Dan and asked him to take me to the prom. Right there at the funeral. Because there's no time to waste, is there? He looked at me as if I'd asked him to cut off an arm for me. And had picked the wrong time and place to ask.

"You don't have a date?" he asked. He was just stalling, I know that now.

"If I had a date, I wouldn't be asking, would I?" But I smiled when I said it.

I didn't like the way he was looking at me. What difference did it make that we were at a funeral? It wasn't as if Leah knew I was arranging my social life on her time.

Then he said he'd asked Megan.

The words hit me like hammers because I hadn't expected them, hadn't expected them at all. He was supposed to be broke, that's what Michael had told me. On one of our nights together, Michael said, "It'll be weird not having Dan at the prom, but he's out of funds and won't be going." He must have been lying, probably, because he was afraid I would ask Dan, (even though he himself was going with Leah). But Michael is a very selfish person, I know that now. He didn't want to share me with Dan.

(Or maybe he was just afraid that if I showed up at the prom I'd say something to Leah. Tell her the truth about her faithless, lying boyfriend.)

Anyway, he lied about Dan being broke, because here was Dan, at the funeral, telling me he was going to the prom with Megan Dunne!

I felt like I'd been hit between the eyes with a bowling ball.

I mumbled something and got away from him.

So of course I had no time left. And now it wasn't just because she was so smart and clever and might come up with answers to questions she had no business asking. Now, she was really in my way.

I guess I can be forgiven for using such crude methods to get rid of her, under the circumstances. I was rushed. There isn't a lot of time left. I haven't done everything that I've done only to end up sitting at home on prom night.

It's not as if I started this whole thing. Leah did, by falling. She's the one who showed me how easy it is to get rid of people who are in my way. She has only herself to blame.

Megan must be ashes by now. Smelly ashes, at that. Ashes . . . dashes . . . smashes . . . crashes.

Tomorrow I'll ask Dan and he'll say yes because Megan can't go with him now. Megan can't go to the prom at all. She can't go anywhere except, oh this is funny, except to the dump. Ouch, laughing makes my headache worse.

I didn't leave a Quartet badge this time. I didn't forget. It just didn't seem appropriate.

I do feel sorry for Adrienne, though. She'll feel bad. And she's nice.

But her daughter shouldn't have got in my way.

Dan had better not be like Michael and say no "out of respect" because Megan's dead. If he does, I don't know what I'll do.

132

Oh, that's a lie. I know exactly what I'll do. Find someone else. There's still a little bit of time left.

And I know exactly where I'll look.

But I'm being silly. I won't have to go hunting again. I'll have Dan.

Sixteen

White . . . so much white . . . white everywhere. On the ceiling, on the walls, on the pale faces of the people looking down upon her. White, white, white. Drowsy with medication, Megan felt a smile slide across her face. "I'm dreaming of a white Christmas," she murmured.

Someone laughed. The laughter was heavy with relief.

But as Megan woke fully, her own smile faded quickly. Her head ached fiercely. Her left knee throbbed. Her eyes felt swollen to twice their normal size, and her entire body was stiff.

One of the very whitest faces belonged to her mother. "Mum, you need blusher in a really bad way," Megan said in that same drowsy tone.

Adrienne laughed, but there were tears in her eyes.

Megan looked up at the rest of the faces. Dan, looking worried. Sophie, biting her lower lip. Jade, her eyes red . . .

from crying? Megan had a vague memory of someone telling her that Jade had been crying. Joseph. Joseph had said that. But Megan couldn't remember why. And there was Lucy, one finger twirling her bright blonde hair.

They all looked so worried.

Megan remembered then. She knew why she was in what had to be a hospital, and she knew why everyone was standing round her looking anxious. The bin. It all flooded back into her mind, a horror film with her as the star. But the medication she'd been given coated the screen with a soft, protective gauze and kept the terror at bay.

There were two other people in the room. One was a tall, skinny man Megan had never seen before. Dressed in a light blue shirt and jeans, he had a beard and glasses and was standing beside the bed, his hand on Megan's right wrist, a stethoscope around his neck. The other person, standing just inside the door, was Dan's brother Eddie, in uniform.

"There's a cop in this room," Megan said. "Why is he here?" She giggled. "Am I going to be arrested for trespassing in that bin?"

"You're a lucky girl," the tall, skinny man said. He used the stethoscope to listen to Megan's chest. "As I understand it, if this young man," pointing to Dan, "hadn't come along, you might not be with us now."

Adrienne moved closer to the bed to take Megan's left hand. "Megan, what happened?" she asked softly.

Megan smiled up at her. "You know that old joke about the housewife in curlers and dressing gown who runs out to the curb and calls to the dustbin men, 'Am I too late for the rubbish?' and the guys on the lorry yell, 'No, jump right in!?'" Megan's eyes closed. "Well, what happened was, I wasn't too late for the rubbish, Mum, so I jumped right in." Then she slipped away into her lovely, gauzy little world.

When she woke again, sun was streaming into the room and she knew that the worst night of her life was over. Her mother and Dan were still in the room. The others had gone, including Officer Eddie McGill. Adrienne was sitting in a straight-backed wooden chair beside the bed. Dan was standing at the wide, uncurtained window, looking out.

A scream of terror slid up into Megan's mouth as she remembered the night before. To stifle it and keep from scaring her mother to death, she quickly told herself she was safe now, here in this hospital room, that the night was over and she shouldn't try right now to figure things out because she was feeling too weak. She would rest here, in this safe place and let people take care of her until she felt better. *Then* she would go over what had happened and try to decide, if that were possible, what it all meant.

"Could I get some breakfast around here?" she asked, sliding up on her pillow. "I'm starving!"

Her mother laughed, and Dan was smiling when he turned away from the window and hurried over to the bed.

"So where'd the long arm of the law go?" Megan smiled at Dan. He looked so worried. "Out catching criminals who toss people into the rubbish bins before their time, I hope."

"Eddie's downstairs having coffee," he answered. "So are your friends. Are you OK?"

"I guess. But I need food and sustenance. So, what about that breakfast?"

Adrienne, smiling with relief, left to see about food for her daughter.

Dan sat down on the foot of Megan's bed. "You look a lot better than the last time I saw you. How's the head? And the knee?" He pointed to a bulge under the white blanket that denoted the thick bandage over Megan's stitches. More than a few stitches, judging by the way her knee felt. She'd have to ask that bearded doctor if she'd be able to dance by prom night.

The prom. Her last thought in the bin returned with dizzying force. But that had been a crazy, nonsensical thought brought on by terror. That's all *that* was. Had to be. Someone wouldn't try to roast her alive just because she was going to a prom.

137

Crazy idea. But then. . .

"Thanks for rescuing me," she told Dan.

He got up, moved to her side, and kissed her. "Thanks for hanging in there," he said seriously. Then he smiled again. "And thanks for not leaving me without a date for the prom."

Megan winced. He was just kidding. He *was*.

"Dr Judge said if you weren't so feisty . . . his word . . . you probably wouldn't have made it. Too much smoke. And you were losing a lot of blood from that cut on your knee."

Smiling, Megan said, "Dr Judge? Isn't that redundant? So, which is he, a doctor or a judge?"

Dan laughed, too, but then said sternly, "Don't change the subject. Are you ready to talk about what happened to you last night? Or do you want to wait for Eddie? I warn you, he's going to have a ton of questions for you."

"Did you see anyone in the alley last night?" Megan asked, settling back on the pillows. Her head had stopped aching, but her knee felt as if it were on fire, like the bin. "Anyone at all?"

He sat back down on the bed. "No. Not a soul. I had to run to the restaurant to get help opening that bin. Someone had jammed a metal file into the lock. Couldn't get it out."

Megan's mother came back into the room, carrying a tray. "It's hospital food," Adrienne apologized, "but I know you. When you're really starving, you'll eat anything."

When Megan had taken a few bites and swallowed, easing

138

the hollow feeling in her stomach, she asked Dan, "Did you know I was in there? In the bin? Or were you just trying to put out the fire?"

"I knew." Remembering made his voice shake slightly. "I saw your shoe. It was on the ground by the bin. The black one? You complained about those shoes at the funeral, said they were too loose, remember? I was looking for you, couldn't find you, and then I smelled and saw the smoke. Ran over to the bin, and there was your shoe, lying right there in front of that flaming mess. So I knew. Listen," his voice shook again, "I almost lost it right then and there. But I didn't. I knew I had to get you out of there. Doc says we did it just in time. A few more minutes. . ." His face went very pale again.

Adrienne shuddered.

But Megan felt a twinge of pride. It had worked. Kicking off the shoe had worked, just as she'd hoped it would. If she hadn't done that, if the shoe hadn't been there, would Dan have known to hunt for her inside the bin? Probably not.

"It was the only thing I could think of doing," she said.

His eyes widened. "You kicked off that shoe on purpose? I thought it fell off."

Megan nodded. "Yep. Last desperate measure, I guess."

"You're one smart cookie," he said admiringly. He glanced over at Adrienne. "This is some clever girl you've raised."

"Yes, I know."

Megan laughed hoarsely. "Not that clever, or I wouldn't have ended up inside that thing, would I?"

"Listen," Dan said, "before you tell us any more, let me go and get Eddie. I can tell that talking hurts your throat, so you shouldn't have to tell the story twice. I'll be right back."

Sophie, Lucy and Jade all trailed along behind Eddie and Dan when they returned. They sat on the floor, and Megan told her story.

She tried to spare her mother the most gruesome details, but now that the medication had worn off, she remembered every moment in such clear detail that when she was finished, Officer McGill had very few questions to ask. She had told him about the saucer of milk and the cat, and his first question when she stopped talking, rubbing her throat, was, "Did you throw that carton out?"

"Yep. It was empty. I put it in the rubbish bag. So it's probably burned to a crisp by now." Why had he asked?

"Maybe not. Not everything in the bin got burned. We'll take a look." When he was satisfied that she'd told him all that she remembered, he folded his notebook, replaced it in his breast pocket, told her to get better quickly, and got up to leave.

"Officer," Megan asked impulsively, "did you . . . well, did you find anything besides my shoe next to the bin?"

He retrieved his notebook, flipped through a few pages, then said, "Nope. Just the shoe." He sent Megan a questioning look. "Why? Should there have been something else there?"

Megan had been thinking of the silver Quartet badges. One had been found on the observation deck at the lighthouse after Leah was attacked. Tonight, just a few days later, Megan had been viciously attacked. So she had half expected McGill to tell her another badge had been found at the bin, making a connection between the two attacks. But she'd been wrong.

Megan wasn't sure whether that was good news or bad news. Either the first badge had meant nothing after all, or the attack on her had no connection to the attack on Leah. How could that be? There couldn't be *two* maniacs loose in Glenview, could there?

"We'll get to the bottom of this," Officer McGill assured her, and left the room.

Dan followed him.

"He's going to ask Eddie how soon they're going to catch the guy who did this," Megan told her mother with a weak smile. As long as her attacker was still out there, she could never feel safe. Never.

"Well, I'd like to know that, too," Adrienne said anxiously. Tears of pain for her daughter's ordeal pricked in her eyes.

Everyone else sat in silence. The horror of what Megan had gone through had stricken them all mute. Finally, Lucy said, "Megan, I can't believe you went through all that! It must have been so terrible."

"Well, I can't believe there's someone like that *out* there!" Sophie exclaimed. "Someone who would do something so horrible. It has to be the same person who killed Leah."

"I'm not so sure," Megan said. "There wasn't any silver Quartet badge. I mean, if that first one, up on the deck, was left there on purpose. There wasn't one this time."

Sophie brushed a lock of frizzy hair aside and said, "Oh, that silly little badge probably didn't mean a thing. Someone just dropped it, that's what I think. Listen, Megan, none of us suspected at first that someone had killed Leah. But now we know that's what happened. The police are sure about that. And we wouldn't have believed that someone would toss you into that bin and set it on fire, but someone did. Those are not rational acts, Megan. Now what are the chances that we've got *two* unbelievably insane people running round loose in Glenview? Doesn't it make more sense that they would be one and the same person?"

Exactly what Megan had been thinking.

Adrienne waved a cautionary hand in the air. "Girls, please, you're upsetting Megan. Could you talk about

142

something else now, please? We can hash this all out later, when the police have found out something. But not now."

Megan knew her mother was still trying to deal with what had happened last night, just as she was. And neither of them had any way of knowing whether or not it was over, did they? "So who's minding the shop, Mum?"

"I closed it. The news about what happened to you is all over town already, so no one will expect us to open today."

"Your silent partners will have a fit. Closing eats into their profits, Mother."

Adrienne smiled. "Think they'll starve?" she asked lightly. "If they're worried about it, they can go down and open Quartet. See what it's like, working for a living." Then she added seriously, "When I do re-open, I'm going to see about some kind of security, Megan. Maybe hire a retired policeman as a watchman, or install an automatic alarm system. I've never thought about it before, because Glenview is so safe . . . *was* so safe. Now, I don't know. I don't think I'll ever feel comfortable about you working alone in the shop again."

"I wasn't *in* the shop, Mum. I was outside."

"I know, but. . ."

The doctor returned, ordering Megan's friends from the room while he examined her again. It allowed Megan the opportunity to ask him the all-important question. "Am I going to be able to dance on this knee in two weeks?"

"Absolutely. No permanent damage. We'll get the stitches out in a week. That'll give you another week to limber up." He listened to Megan's chest again, nodded with satisfaction and said, "I heard about the shoe. Good thinking. I have a feeling that if you really want to dance in two weeks, young lady, you'll dance."

When he left, her friends returned, and Adrienne went downstairs for coffee.

"I can't believe you're smiling," Lucy said. "You must be just sick about missing the prom." She was wearing a bright yellow T-shirt, which reminded Megan, with a sickening lurch of her stomach, of Leah, floating . . . Megan pushed the ugly thought away.

"Well, I would be if I were going to miss it," she said. "But I'm not. The doctor was just here. He says I'll be fine in plenty of time."

"That can't be right," Lucy protested. She had plopped down on the white tiled floor. Sophie sat beside her, nervously fingering the straps on her bag. Jade, her blue flowered skirt spread out around her, had taken a seat on the window-sill. "Dan said your knee was a bloody mess," Lucy continued. "So we were sure you'd be missing the prom. Now you say you're still going. How can you possibly dance on it so soon?"

"That would be stupid, Megan," Jade agreed. "If you put that much stress on a knee that was cut practically to the bone, you could end up crippled or something."

"I think Megan should go to the prom and dance up a storm," Sophie disagreed quietly. "If the doctor says she can, then she can. She'd be crazy not to go. *I'd* do it – if I had the chance."

"Yeah," Lucy said, sighing, "who are we kidding? We all would, knee or no knee."

"Well, *I* wouldn't!" Jade cried, jumping up from the sill. "But if Megan wants to risk crippling herself over some stupid, silly dance, I guess that's her business, isn't it? I just thought she was smarter than that!" And she stalked out of the room, her head high.

But Megan had seen the tears sparkling on Jade's lower lashes. She thought about mentioning Joseph's phone call about Jade to the others, but decided not to. If *she* were Jade, she wouldn't want anyone to know that someone was calling her friends to tell them she'd been crying her eyes out.

"So," Megan said with artificial brightness, "did you guys do anything exciting last night?"

"I hit the books," Sophie said. "I wanted to see a film, but no one else did. Jade studied, too, but she didn't want to get together to do it. She said she thinks better alone. Me, I like company when I'm trying to memorize. It helps if they quiz me. So," waving a hand towards Lucy, "I talked our friend here into grilling me."

Megan reached for a glass of water on her bedside table. "Did it work?"

"I won't know for sure until the exams. Anyway, Lucy didn't stay very long."

Lucy shrugged. "I was so tired. That horrible funeral yesterday, and then that horrendous time at Leah's house. Everyone was crying and it was just such a bummer. I was glad to get out of there. Poor Michael. He's not even going to the prom. He's taking his exams early and leaving to spend the summer with his uncle. I think he feels guilty about not treating Leah better than he did. He's taking her death really hard. So are her friends. Beth didn't say a word to anyone except Michael yesterday, and Zoe looked like she was still in shock, and Lily never stopped crying."

"I noticed you did your best to cheer up Michael," Sophie said dryly.

"Like you didn't? If you weren't hoping he'd change his mind about leaving before the prom, I'll eat one of those Quartet badges."

Sophie laughed. "You can't. You lost yours."

"You lost yours, too. But there are more at the shop."

"Everyone loses them," Megan said. "They're cheap. The catches don't work very well." That reminded her of the badge found on the lighthouse deck. "Have the police found out anything more about who might have pushed Leah off the lighthouse deck?" If they caught *that* person, wouldn't they also be catching the maniac who had thrown her into that bin and set it on fire? Then she'd be safe again.

"Not that we've heard." Lucy stood up. "Listen, we've got to go to the decorating committee meeting. Sorry you can't make it. But there's one tomorrow afternoon, too, and one on Wednesday. We'll keep you posted with what goes on. Can we bring you anything if we come back tonight?"

"Something to read, maybe. I'm being let out tomorrow, so don't make it *War and Peace*, OK? Maybe a magazine." Although it would be impossible to concentrate on reading anything.

Sophie stood up, too. "You're being released tomorrow? I thought they'd keep you here a lot longer. I mean, with the smoke inhalation and your cracked skull. . ."

"I heal fast. I might even make it to the meeting. Now go and find Jade and cheer her up, OK? She's really upset about the prom."

Sophie's thin face twisted with cynicism. "You're asking us to help? Isn't that like asking someone who's never skied to teach you how to slalom? We can't even get dates for ourselves."

"I didn't say you had to find her a date. I said, cheer her up. You can do that. Make her laugh."

They promised, but Megan wasn't expecting much. It would take more than a little joking around to cheer up Jade.

How could *anyone* in Glenview be cheerful these days? Wasn't everyone having nightmares? Glenview had always been so peaceful, so safe. Until now. . .

Megan hoped the doctor had ordered medication for later, after visiting hours. A pill or an injection that would keep her own nightmares away. She hadn't a shred of hope that they wouldn't be there, lying in wait for her the second she closed her eyes. Even in the bright sunshine of daytime, she kept feeling those cold hands on her ankles again, felt herself being lifted up, and thrown into that greasy, smelly mess, felt the heat from the fire.

Even though she was in one piece, even though she hadn't died like Leah, she would be reliving last night's terrible experience for many nights to come.

Seventeen

Megan's room was busy with activity all evening. She welcomed the company. As exhausted as she was, she was grateful for the distraction. It helped keep the demons of shock and fear at bay.

Jade returned during visiting hours with Sophie and Lucy. She apologized for her earlier outburst, but Megan could still feel the tension in the air.

I know what she wants, Megan found herself thinking as Jade and Lucy began discussing Leah's death and how weird it was that her dress had been taken from Quartet after she died. Jade wants me to say I won't go to the prom if she's not going. She wants me to say: *We've always spent prom night together, having fun, and since this is our very last prom night at Glenview, I want things to be like they've always been. I want you to spend it with the rest of us.*

But I'm not going to say that, Megan vowed. Jade could be

going, too, if she weren't so stubborn. And then prom night would be different for both of us, but it would be a *good* kind of different.

"What I want to know is," Sophie said, "who polishes shoes to wear to a picnic? The cops said they found black shoe polish in those cuts and scratches on Leah's knuckles. I don't *know* anyone who polishes their shoes. Most of us wear trainers ninety per cent of the time."

"Lily Pappas would wear shoes that need polishing," Lucy said. "And she'd make absolutely sure they were shining like the sun before she took one step outside, even if it was only to a picnic."

Megan found herself nodding agreement. Lily was Glenview's fashion queen. She wore the most expensive, stylish clothes and her outfits were always perfectly coordinated right down to her shoes, belt and jewellery.

"That's crazy, " Sophie said. "Lily was one of Leah's best friends. Why would she kill her?"

"How should I know? I don't have any special insight into the criminal mind," Lucy said.

Megan remembered Dan telling her that the police always looked to the closest person to any murder victim . . . a spouse, a relative. Would "close" include best friend?

Of course it would. In high school, who was closer than a best friend?

Impossible to imagine cool, beautiful Lily committing as vicious an act as the one that had taken Leah's life.

But then, Megan told herself, everything that's happened would have been impossible to imagine just a few days ago. Being locked in a rubbish bin? It would never occur to any rational human being that such an obscene thing could actually happen. If she hadn't *been* there, she wouldn't believe it herself.

Her friends had barely left the room when they were replaced by a trio whose arrival was so stunning, Megan was rendered speechless. She was glancing through the magazine that Jade had brought her when a voice said, "Can we come in, Megan?"

She looked up to find the Pops standing in the doorway smiling at her. Zoe was carrying a small white wicker basket filled with flowers, Lily a box of chocolates, and Beth a magazine.

Megan was so shocked, she almost burst out with, "You don't look the same without Leah in the middle." It was true. They didn't. They had been a quartet. Now they were a trio. But pointing that out would be too cruel.

When she did find her tongue, all she could manage was, "Oh. Hi. Sure. Come on in." She could not believe they had come to see her. What on earth were Pops doing in her room?

"We were worried about you," Zoe said, plopping down

on the window-sill and handing Megan the flowers. They were beautiful. "We don't want poor Daniel to end up alone on prom night. But he promised us that you're going to be fine in plenty of time."

She'd been talking to Dan? Megan felt a pang of jealousy, and then reminded herself that the two were just friends.

"You know, Megan," Beth said solemnly, "when we first heard, we were afraid the same thing that happened to Leah had happened to you. We were so relieved when Dan told us you were OK. He did say you were hurt. But OK. Not . . . not like Leah. How are you feeling?" She lay the magazine on the bed. "I read it first," she apologized. "Hope you don't mind."

"Of course I don't. And I'm feeling fine." Megan's left hand moved without her consent to her hair to try and push some life into it. All three girls looked so perfect. How did they *do* that? Every shining blonde hair in place on Zoe's head, Lily's make-up perfectly applied on her smooth, olive skin, Beth's slender frame model-perfect in an expensive tight dress. So much perfection.

Megan half expected one of them to open her mouth and say, "Please don't hate me because I'm beautiful."

Her discomfort had nothing to do with her physical condition. What was she going to talk to these people about? She had absolutely nothing in common with any of them. Except Dan. And she wasn't about to discuss Dan with them.

152

She began leafing idly through the magazine Beth had brought her. "I'm going home tomorrow," she said, because she couldn't think of anything else to say. Now that she was going to the prom, she could talk about that, but she didn't feel like it. Not with them. It would sound too much like the novice consulting the old pros. Yuck.

"Already?" Beth asked. "Isn't that awfully soon? Dan explained what you went through. And then it was on the news, in graphic detail. It sounded so horrible, Megan. You could have died in that bin."

Megan shifted in her bed. "I'm fine. Really. I'll be at the meeting."

Zoe frowned. "The decorating committee meeting? Oh, Megan, really, that's silly. You should rest tomorrow." She smiled. "We'll take care of Dan for you, if that's what you're worried about. I know he's going to be there. You know, we asked him to be on the committee and he said he didn't have time. I guess you have more influence over him than any of us."

I guess I do, Megan thought.

"I'll be at the meeting," she said firmly. Her eyes on the magazine in her lap, she scanned an article about dressing for success and turned the page. To find a drawing nestled among the pages.

Drawn on plain white paper, it was a coloured pencil

sketch of a girl with long, yellow hair in a slender blue dress. It was, quite clearly, meant to be Beth. She was carrying a huge bouquet of red flowers in her arms. Wearing a large, golden crown on her head. And she was smiling from ear to ear.

Megan glanced up at Beth, whose face had turned a painful scarlet. Lily and Zoe were engaged in conversation and hadn't noticed the drawing.

Please, Beth's blue eyes pleaded, please don't show them.

Megan quickly turned the page. Beth wanted to be queen?

Well, why not? Didn't every girl at Glenview High? Lily and Zoe had already been crowned. Why not Beth?

But Megan wondered if there wasn't something a little bizarre about a girl sitting somewhere alone drawing a picture of herself wearing a crown. It gave her an eerie feeling.

"Thanks for the magazine," was all she said to Beth as the girls left.

Two minutes later, Beth came hurrying back in, her cheeks red. "I told them I had to go to the ladies," she said, moving to stand beside Megan's bed. "Listen, about the drawing. . ."

Megan waved a hand. "Forget it. I'm not into sharing. Don't worry."

"No, I . . . I wanted to explain. You must think I'm crazy or something. It's just . . . well, I never told any of my friends this, but I really would like to be queen of our last prom at Glenview. Jordan is a lot more popular than I am, like Leah was. He should be king. If he were going with Leah, he would be. Anyway, I was just daydreaming in school the other day, and the drawing just sort of happened. Could I have it back now?"

Megan leafed through the magazine, found the drawing, and handed it to Beth. But she was wondering exactly *when* Beth had taken up art. Before Leah fell off that deck? Or after? "My lips are sealed," she said to Beth. "And good luck, I think you'd make a great queen."

"Thanks, Megan." Crumpling up the drawing and tossing it into Megan's wastebasket, Beth hurried out of the room.

Megan still didn't understand why the Pops had come to see her, and wondered if Dan had sent them.

"Nope, I had nothing to do with it," he claimed later when he was sitting beside her bed. "They must have come on their own."

Megan didn't tell him that, as they were leaving, she had checked out Lily's shoes. They had indeed been black, and were the kind of expensive leather shoes that would probably need polishing.

That might have meant something if it weren't for one other inescapable fact. Megan couldn't say for sure that Lily was not a killer. She didn't know her well enough. But she *could* say for sure that, like Leah Markham, Lily Pappas would never, in a million years, have worn one of the cheap silver Quartet badges. So, while Megan had no idea whose badge had been found on the observation deck of the lighthouse, she knew it wasn't Lily's.

That still didn't mean she hadn't had one in her possession, dropping it on the deck as some kind of message after Leah had fallen.

But then, why hadn't there been one next to the rubbish bin?

"Any news from Eddie?" she asked Dan.

He regarded her with mock cynicism. "Is that the only reason you're hanging out with me? So I can feed you information about the investigations? There *are* two of them now, you know," he added. "Leah's, and yours. Three, if you count that business with the dresses at the shop."

"Yes," Megan said with a perfectly straight face, "that is the *only* reason I'm the least bit interested in you. Why else? You are ugly and boring and a complete turn-off."

"Liar," he said, grinning, and bent to kiss her.

She was discharged the following morning. Adrienne had the fit that Megan had expected when her daughter announced shortly after her arrival home that she was planning to attend the decorating committee meeting that afternoon.

"I can't believe that meeting hasn't been cancelled!" Megan's mother led her to the sofa, insisting that she lie down. "You girls are just not safe out there right now. I don't know what's going on, but I will *not* have you wandering around town without protection, Megan. Not after what you've been through. Not until the police have some answers."

"I'm not going to be wandering around, Mother. I'll be in the school gym. There will be lots of other people there, including Dan. In fact, he's picking me up and bringing me home. So I'll be perfectly safe." She really believed that, or she would never have considered leaving her house. That . . . *person* . . . was still out there. But she wouldn't be alone, so she wouldn't be a target if he or she decided Sunday afternoon was a good time to finish the job.

"Megan," Adrienne said, sitting down on the edge of the sofa, "I came very close to losing you on Friday night." Her hands shook as she covered Megan's legs with a blanket, and her voice was heavy with emotion. "You're all I have. I couldn't. . ." Her voice broke, making it impossible for her to continue.

"Mum, it's OK," Megan said quietly, patting her mother's hand. "I promise you I will not take one single step alone today, OK? I promise! I really want to go to this meeting, especially now that I'm actually going to the prom. You *wanted* me to go, remember?"

"That was before. . ."

"I'll be at *school*," Megan pleaded, really worried now that her mother wasn't going to give in this time. "Nothing bad has happened at school. And when I get home, we'll talk about where to go from here. I agree with you that working alone at the shop is a definite no-no, and I have no intention of going anywhere near the Point. But I have to go to school during the week, anyway. So why can't I go there today? I promise I'll rest right here on this sofa until it's time to go. I won't move a muscle."

"All right," her mother said reluctantly. "I really don't want to spoil this time for you, you know that. But Megan, I've never been as frightened in my life as I was when Dan came racing into the restaurant and shouted that the bin was on fire and you'd been trapped inside. He couldn't get it open. I will never forget that, as long as I live."

"I'm sorry you had to go through that. Look, I'll call you from the meeting, OK? Every five minutes, if you want. Every *minute*."

Adrienne laughed. It was weak, but better than nothing. "You don't have to do that. But . . . you could call at least once, just to say that things are going OK. Will Mrs Thompson be there?"

Mrs Thompson. An old crone if ever there was one, sour-faced and tight-lipped. But a teacher was required, and she was the only one willing to spend the time. "I'm sure she will be. She was there the last three times."

"All right, then." Adrienne sighed. "I know I can't keep you locked up in the house, although that's what my maternal instincts tell me to do. Come right home after the meeting?"

"I promise. I'll be back by five. Don't worry, OK?"

Megan went to the meeting. She went with a queasy stomach, a slight headache, a stiff knee, and constant glances over her shoulder, but she did go.

She only hoped, as she climbed awkwardly into Dan's car, that she wasn't making a terrible mistake leaving the safety of her home.

Eighteen

She's not dead! Not even close. What rotten luck!

I can't figure out how it happened. Oh, I know Dan dragged her out of there in time, but how did he know she was in there? If he got there in time to see the smoke and maybe flames coming out of the bin, why didn't he just call the fire brigade? What made him think to look for her inside the thing? She couldn't have been screaming . . . too much smoke. Wasn't even making much noise while I was still there. I could hear how hard it was for her to breathe, so by that time I wasn't worried about her screaming loud enough to attract anyone's attention.

So how did he know she was in there?

There she was, sitting up in that hospital bed like a queen. She couldn't actually be prom queen, could she? I'd say absolutely not, except that Dan is such a big deal at school, maybe people will suddenly like her just because she's with him. That would kill me.

I cannot believe she's still alive. And healthy enough to go. She'll probably even be able to dance.

I should have taken the time to plan more carefully.

Still, they don't know about the other part yet. The evidence should be ashes. If it's not, I'll deal with that later.

Right now, I have to decide what to do. I'm not giving up. But everyone's going to be watching her to see that nothing else happens. I won't be able to get at her.

OK, this is what I need to do. First I'll make sure I've got someone waiting in the wings, just in case my plans for Megan are thwarted. I'll take care of that part of it tomorrow. I'm not missing the prom because of Dan McGill. Anyone is better than no one.

But he's the one I really want. He's the best choice.

Now I think about it, maybe tomorrow's little distraction will take some of that attention away from Megan, leaving her more vulnerable. So I can swoop in for the kill.

The kill . . . that's pretty funny.

But my head aches too much to laugh.

Nineteen

When they got to the gym, Megan and Dan split up. He left to help Jordan and David borrow a ladder from the caretakers. The Pops were seated at a long, narrow table along one side, armed with notebooks and paper. Megan felt their stares as she stood in the gym doorway. And when she passed their table to join Jade, Sophie, and Lucy, busy unpacking boxes of tiny ceramic yearbooks in green and white, Glenview High's colours, Beth sent her a nervous glance. Megan simply nodded.

Jade barely looked up when Megan joined them. Had Joseph told her about his phone call? Jade would be embarrassed by that.

Megan split the tape open on the box in front of her. "Who's taking Leah's place as chairperson?"

"Lily." Jade glanced over at the Pops' table. "The Pops picked her, of course. She's taken complete control, complaining about everything. I frankly do not understand what David Goumas sees in that girl. She's still arguing about the theme, saying it should be Tropical Nights, which anyone with a brain knows has been done to death, instead of Happy Endings, which is much more appropriate since we're about to graduate, right? And then she said. . ."

Megan wasn't really listening. The guys had returned with the ladder, and Zoe and Lily had gathered round them, giving orders. Megan's eyes were on Zoe. She really was gorgeous, even in jeans and a long-sleeved white shirt. The guys at Glenview must all be devastated that Zoe was going to the prom with a college guy. Who wouldn't want someone who looked like Zoe at his side on such a special night?

No matter how my mother fusses with my hair and make-up on prom night, Megan thought despondently, I am never going to look anything like Zoe Buffet. Never.

Never mind, she told herself briskly, you're not only going, you're going with someone really nice. Who apparently *didn't* want Zoe at his side. He wanted you. So shut up about how you're going to look, OK? You'll look fine.

". . .and then Lily said we hadn't ordered nearly enough candles and so I'm supposed to get myself over to the mall this afternoon to buy more, but she hasn't given me any money. If she thinks I'm going to spend my own hard-earned cash on candles for a prom I'm probably not even going to go to, she can think again." Out of breath at last, Jade paused, but only for a moment. "Megan? You're not listening, are you? What's the matter with you? Are you feeling ill? Or are you still angry with us for going to Leah's house after the funeral? Not that it did us any good," she added gloomily. "Who would have thought that Michael Danz would miss his own senior prom?"

Megan didn't say what she was thinking. That Michael Danz was probably avoiding the prom out of guilt, not sadness. Did the girl he'd been seeing feel the same guilt? "Sorry. I was just wondering about Leah's dress. Who could have taken it? How did they get into the shop? What did they do with it?"

"Oh, let's not talk about that stuff now, OK?" Lucy carefully unwrapped another tiny yearbook. "It's too creepy. I can't believe your mother let you come to this meeting, Megan. After what happened. I thought she'd lock you in your room until the police found that guy. My own mother nearly had a fit when I told her I was leaving the house. She's terrified that I'm going to end up like Leah."

"All the parents in Glenview probably are. Getting out of the house did take some doing," Megan admitted. "But Mum's so excited about me going to the prom, she thought I should be in on the decorating, so here I am."

"I have to go to the mall and get those candles," Jade said, turning away from Megan. "But first, I need to get the money from Lily."

Megan felt a twinge of disappointment. She had hoped they would talk about her invitation to the prom, at least a little. It was exciting, and she wanted to share that excitement with her friends. But they all seemed to be avoiding the subject.

Well, what did you expect? she asked herself as she followed Jade over to Lily's table. You're breaking up the quartet that planned to celebrate together on prom night, just like always. If one of them had a date instead of you, would *you* be rejoicing?

No, Megan answered honestly, probably not.

"I don't have the money *on* me," Lily retorted when Jade asked her for the funds. "I don't carry it around. It's in Mrs Thompson's desk drawer. Her *locked* desk drawer, of course. I've been very careful with that money. Thompson's out of town at a wedding, that's why she's not here." Lily tossed her short, silky dark hair. "But I have a key to the drawer."

Mrs Thompson's classroom was on the fourth floor.

Jade made a small sound of protest. "You don't have the money with you? It'll take you forever to go all the way up to the fourth floor. It's not like this high school has a lift, Lily. It's already past three. I want to get to the mall and back this *year*."

"I'm not going by way of China, Jess. That *is* your name, isn't it?"

Jade's cheeks flamed. "No, it's Jade."

"Sorry. Look. I'll be right back, I promise." Lily stood up, stuck a pencil behind one ear. "I might take a minute in the ladies, see if I can't do something with this hair." Her hair looked perfect. She hesitated and then mused aloud, "Maybe I should take David with me. I know nothing creepy has happened here at school, and maybe I'm being silly, but roaming round the halls alone might not be such a hot idea right now."

She walked confidently over to David, who was adjusting the ladder, and said something to him. His handsome face creased into a frown, and he shook his head no. Lily argued briefly, then turned away, annoyed.

"I guess I'm on my own," she said when she came back, shrugging. To Jade, she said, "Just relax, Jess, OK? I'm sending you to the mall, not the moon. Stop looking so worried. I promise I'll hurry." Lily turned and walked quickly, confidently, out of the gym, apparently having forgotten that she'd had misgivings about leaving the room alone.

"My name isn't Jess!" Jade called angrily. "It's Jade!"

"Whatever." Lily waved a careless hand over one shoulder and disappeared round a corner.

Megan could see that Jade was fuming. She walked over to

her and said, "It'll take her a few minutes. Let's go and sit outside while we wait. It's gorgeous out, and I need some air. I can't stand the smell of gym socks another second."

"No thanks. I'm going to my locker. I forgot my physics book and I need to study tonight." Then she looked at Megan, her gaze level. "Why don't you see if Dan will go with you? I'm sure he'd love to."

Oh, Jade, Megan thought, don't be like that. But she said nothing. The truth was, at that moment she *would* rather be sitting outside with Dan. He'd be better company than Jade in the mood she was in.

Everyone took advantage of the break. There were quick trips to lockers, visits to the ladies, treks in search of a drinking fountain or vending machine. Dan, Jordan, David, and two other boys on the committee went outside to toss a ball around.

Megan went outside, too. The sun was warm, comforting, the air fresh. She hadn't slept very well the night before and her knee was aching. When she sat down on one of the wide, stone steps and leaned back against a fat white pillar, she closed her eyes and dozed off.

She was snapped back to reality by the sound of Sophie's voice from inside the gym. "Hey, where is everybody? We're going to be here all night if we don't get back to work."

Megan roused herself, shook her head, stretched. and

167

called out to the ball players, who had moved out of sight in search of a grassy stretch of lawn.

But when they all moved back inside the gym, only Sophie was standing at the table littered with decorating supplies.

Jordan looked indignant, asking Megan accusingly, "How come you made us come back inside when no one else is here?"

"Oh, thanks a lot!" Sophie sent Jordan an insulted look.

"You know what I mean. Lily's not here with the money. I'm going back outside. Call me when she gets here."

But before they could turn round and leave the gym again, Beth and Zoe, then Jade, entered the big room. Lucy arrived a few seconds later, her arms full of books. "So, let's get started," Sophie said impatiently, plopping her skinny frame into a chair. She glanced up at Beth. "What are we supposed to do next?"

"Don't ask me. I'm clueless. We'll have to wait until Lily gets back. She'll give Jade the candle money, Jade will go to the mall, and while she's gone, we'll do whatever Lily has on her list. But first, we need her. I think we should just wait."

So everyone sat in the metal folding chairs around the long, narrow, metal table in the warm, sunlit gym and waited for Lily.

But Lily didn't come back.

Twenty

Lily Pappas hurried along the scuffed wooden floor that now, in late May, no longer smelled of fresh varnish, as it had in September. She hated that smell. It reminded her every autumn that an entire new year of school was beginning, another nine long months of long days striving to Get It Right.

Lily chewed on her lower lip. So many things to remember when it came to getting it right. Looking Good, that came first, of course. That was never enough, though. After that came Good Grades and then Talent and if you managed all of it properly, you became Popular, which was the goal all along, right?

It was all very hard work and she had no reason to believe it would get any easier in college. Might even be harder. There'd be more competition, for one thing.

She didn't have to worry about competition when it came

169

to dating. That was always a comforting thought. She had David. He really loved her. And they were going to the same university. One of the best, of course. Zoe and Beth would be there, too, because like most best friends, they had made a pact years and years ago that they wouldn't be separated. Leah had been part of the pact. It wouldn't be the same without her.

Lily rounded a corner in the hallway, thinking, but first, before college, there's the prom. The best night of the year. She loved proms. She'd gone to every single one in high school.

And Dan had asked that girl Megan, who had almost died on Friday night. A horrible, terrible thing, almost as bad as Leah dying. Scary stuff. Very scary stuff.

But Dan and Megan Dunne? What was *that* all about? Trying to make Zoe jealous? But Zoe *wasn't* jealous. Why should she be? She was going with a college guy. It was Lily's opinion that Zoe had outgrown high school guys a long time ago. She was just too clever and sophisticated for most of them. In truth, she probably scared them half to death. Zoe would sparkle in college. She belonged there. Leah would have, too, only. . .

Tears stung Lily's eyes. She and Leah had argued. Often. But they'd never stopped being best friends. Losing Leah was like having an arm or a leg removed. She would never get used to her not being there.

Lily rounded another corner, this one leading to the fourth floor hallway outside Mrs Thompson's room. Taking Leah's place as chairperson of the prom committee was definitely a feather in her cap. The prom was a very big deal. But in all honesty, she would rather have Leah back. No one would believe that, but it was true. It was absolutely, painfully true.

Stepping carefully, Lily moved to Mrs Thompson's classroom, unlocked the door, and went inside. She knew exactly which desk drawer held the metal box containing the prom funds. When it was sitting on top of the desk, she bent to re-lock the drawer, and just then heard a soft, padding sound behind her. She smiled. David. He had decided it wasn't safe for her to be running round up here all alone, after all, and he'd followed to make sure she was all right.

But the smile was short-lived. Because in the next second, before she had a chance to turn round or say, "David?" a hand reached around from behind her, lifted the box, grasped the metal handle, and slammed the heavy metal box into Lily's face so hard, the handle broke and the box fell to the floor. Lily, lifted off her feet by the force of the blow, sailed backwards three metres before collapsing on the floor, blood pouring from her shattered nose and a deep gash on her upper lip.

Hands reached down, snatched up the box, lifted it

overhead and would have brought it down once again on the fallen girl's skull. But voices sounding in the distance interrupted the motion.

"Good enough," a voice said over Lily's head. Hands lowered the box. "You won't be taking *that* face to the prom. Sorry about this, Lily, but you have something I need. A prom date."

The box containing the prom funds left the room in the hands of Lily's attacker.

On the classroom floor, Lily Pappas continued to lie, bloody and silent, on the wooden floor that no longer smelled of varnish.

Twenty-One

"This is ridiculous!" Lucy said crankily. "We are wasting so much time. I have better things to do than sit here waiting for Lily forever." She smiled coyly at David. "I'll go with you if you want to see what's taking her so long."

Megan rolled her eyes and said, "Maybe she couldn't get the door open. Or the drawer where Mrs Thompson was keeping the money. Lucy's right. We should go and see what's up." Because, she thought with a sudden skip in her pulse, the last time someone was missing. . .

She refused to finish the thought. Lily wasn't missing. She just hadn't come back into the gym yet.

But then Beth stood up and said quietly, "I don't like this. I have a funny feeling."

Lily's boyfriend, David, stared at her. "What? *What*?"

"I don't know." Beth's fair-skinned face went whiter. "I just have this feeling." She moved away from the table. "Can we please go upstairs and get Lily?"

"She's right," Zoe said, her voice strained. "She's been gone too long."

"Why not?" Dan agreed, his voice light and casual. Megan was sure that he was making an effort to ease the sudden, eerie tension that Beth's remarks had created. "It's better than sitting around here growing cobwebs."

"We could still be playing ball," Jordan complained, but his mouth looked tense and he stood up, too.

No one else uttered a word as everyone in the gym headed for the stairs.

More than once on the way up, negotiating the stairs with difficulty because of her knee, Megan felt Zoe's and Beth's eyes scrutinizing her, as if they were trying to figure out what Dan saw in her.

Big deal, Megan told herself. I'm not going with *them*. The truth was, it still hadn't sunk in that she was going to the prom. All she'd been thinking about was how lucky she was to be alive. But she *was* going, and with Dan McGill. Shouldn't she be shouting it from the roof of the school?

It was hard to shout joy from the rooftops when someone had just died and she herself had almost done the same. And now Lily wasn't where she should have been.

The bump on Megan's head began to throb again.

What they saw as they turned the final corner into Mrs Thompson's classroom was two caretakers in grey overalls bending over a limp body. Even from the end of the hall they could see vivid red around her. Red that shouldn't have been there. Red spilling down over her face into a liquid pool beneath her head.

"Oh, oh, no," Beth breathed. "I knew it, I *knew* it!" No one else uttered a sound.

One of the two men was just leaving to summon help. As he passed the group, he told them quickly, "It's not as bad as it looks. Don't let all that blood scare you." Then he hurried off to find a telephone.

Lily had just begun to stir when they arrived at her side. What they saw was not a pretty sight.

Everyone standing round her in a semicircle sucked in their breath when they saw the damage. David was the first to speak. "Oh, man," he groaned in a low, stunned voice, "look at her face!" He fell to his knees at Lily's side.

"What happened to her?" Beth asked, her voice trembling as she, too, knelt beside Lily. "Did she fall?"

Lily opened her eyes. Both were already swelling and beginning to turn purple. Blood oozed from the nasty cut on her upper lip. But the worst damage had been done to her nose. Her perfect nose, broken now, a lumpy, swollen mass of cartilage and bones, still bleeding profusely. The eyes closed again, possibly because it hurt to keep them open.

"Doesn't look to me like she just fell," the other caretaker said. "Looks to me like she got clobbered, with something pretty heavy. George isn't just calling an ambulance. He's calling the police, too."

"Where's the money?" Jade asked sharply. "I don't see any cash box or envelope around here anywhere."

The man at Lily's side glanced up. "Money? What money?"

Lucy waved towards the desk. "She came up here to get our prom money. But I can't see it here anywhere. I hate to be crass, but the prom isn't going to be cancelled just because Lily smashed her face in, so there are still things to do. The key is still in the drawer. Maybe she didn't have time to take the box out. I'll have a look." She did, and when she turned round again, her expression was grim. "It's not here. She was hit *after* she took the box out." She returned to the group. "We need to know where that money is. *Before* they cart her off to hospital."

"That *is* crass," Zoe snapped. No one else said anything.

Jade and Jordan checked the hallway for any sign of a metal cash box or an envelope. They found neither.

"It doesn't *matter*," Beth cried when the pair returned to the group empty-handed. "We'll find that stuff later. *Where is* that ambulance? The bleeding hasn't stopped. She could. . ."

Lily's eyes opened again. "What's the matter?" she murmured through swollen lips. "What's wrong with me? My face hurts." Then she added, still murmuring, "Someone hit me. Wasn't David . . . wasn't."

Beth leaned closer. "What? What did you say, Lily? Did you see someone? Who was it?"

"A voice. Telling me." Lily closed her eyes again.

The wail of an ambulance approached the school.

"What voice?" Beth asked, flinching as she looked down upon Lily's battered face. "I don't understand."

Megan didn't, either. For the second time that week, she was looking at a face that, just a short while ago, had been beautiful. Not a mark on it. Nothing to mar its perfection. But not now. Far from it. Even with the blood wiped away, Lily Pappas was not going to look like herself for quite some time.

Everyone waited in silence while the paramedics checked Lily's condition. "She's stable," one of them finally said. "No serious damage done. Needs repair work on the nose, though, and she could have concussion. She must have taken quite a blow. One of you call her parents, tell them to meet us at casualty."

David rushed away to make the call.

The paramedics carefully loaded Lily onto a stretcher. The minute they picked her up, Megan saw the badge. It had been lying underneath Lily's arm. A silver quartet badge.

She bent to pick it up, then wondered if it might have fingerprints and decided to leave it there.

She moved over to stand beside Dan, pointing to the badge. "Do you see that?"

But before he could answer, two police officers arrived. They questioned the paramedics briefly, then turned towards the silent, white-faced group.

Another badge, Megan was thinking as the officers approached. Just like on the deck. But there hadn't been one outside the rubbish bin. Why not?

The paramedics finished strapping Lily in and picked up the stretcher. No one said anything. Lily looked so awful. Her nose had swollen to twice its normal size, forcing her eyes shut. But she was not unconscious. "I wanted to go to the prom," she said softly as the stretcher was lifted.

Hearing her, Megan recognized her own final thought just before she'd passed out in the bin. Badge or no badge outside that bin, the same person who had done this terrible thing to Lily had attacked her on Friday night. And Lily's remarks just now told her beyond any doubt that Jade had been right, as usual. It *was* about the prom. A ridiculous, stupid, insane idea, but Megan knew it was the truth.

Someone was trying to sabotage the prom. Why? Hoping it would be cancelled? Why would someone want that? Because they weren't going?

An obscene idea. Or was the correct word *insane*?

The scarier thought that immediately followed that one was, maybe it wasn't the prom itself the attacker was targeting. Maybe it was only people who were *going* to the prom. Why would someone do that? Because he or she *wasn't* going and was angry about it? Or was that much too simplistic? People had been missing out on high school proms for years and years and as far as Megan knew, they didn't go around killing the luckier ones.

She reminded herself grimly that she was now a member of that group. The lucky group. The ones who *were* going.

When she quietly told Dan what she was thinking, he asked if she actually thought someone could really care that much that they weren't going.

She said no, of course not. She was tired and she had a headache and she wasn't thinking clearly. But even to her own ears, that didn't sound very convincing.

She wanted, more than anything, to be wrong about what she was thinking. She didn't want Leah's death, her own attack in the alley, or this newest attack on Lily to have anything to do with the prom. Selfish of her, maybe, but the thought that the dance she had waited so long to attend could be the reason for all this ugliness was just too depressing.

"I'd just like to remind all of you," Lucy announced when

the stretcher had disappeared round a corner, "that the funds Mrs Thompson was keeping for us weren't just for candles. That money was for everything: the decorations, the caterer, food and drink, the band, the flowers, everything. Shouldn't we be trying to figure out what happened to it? We're going to need that money."

"I don't see what choice we have," Zoe said. "We'll have to wait and find out from Lily when she's feeling better. That won't be until tomorrow. I'm sorry if that disturbs you, but we can't help it."

Lucy stunned Megan then by smiling sweetly at David and saying earnestly, "I'm sorry. Zoe is right. I've been callous. I really was thinking of all of you, though. I mean, *I'm* not going. I haven't been asked yet. But you guys are going. I just don't want you to be disappointed, that's all."

Megan glared at her. Since when did Lucy Dowd care if the Pops were disappointed about something? She hadn't already set her sights on David, had she? With Lily not even at the hospital yet?

The police seemed to feel the incident was a simple robbery. Their scenario involved someone passing by the room as Lily lifted the cash box out of the drawer. The thief had hit her with the heavy box, then escaped with the money.

Megan pointed out the silver badge. But there were too many people around willing to assert, just as they had at the lighthouse, that the badges were common. No significance there, she read in the officers' faces.

They said they would talk to "the victim". But Megan felt they'd already made up their minds about what had happened.

On their way out of the building in the late afternoon sun, Megan hissed at Lucy, "*What* were you doing back there? Flirting with David? I could swear that's what you were doing, but I *have* to be wrong, don't I? Because you couldn't possibly have been."

Lucy shrugged. "You know Lily would never show that face in public. She's too vain. She's not going to look normal in time for the prom. My uncle broke his nose once when I was little, and I was afraid to go near him, he looked so awful. As far as I know, David has never cheated on Lily, like Michael did on Leah. But even if he were willing to take her to the prom looking as if she's just done ten rounds with a boxing champion, she'd never go. So," she added cheerfully, "he needs a date if he's going to attend his senior prom, right, Megan?"

Megan was about to say, "Forget David, Lucy. If Lily doesn't go, David won't, either," when the silver Quartet van suddenly pulled up at the foot of the steps and screeched to a halt. Adrienne jumped out, her eyes on the ambulance pulling away from the curb, her face grey. She hadn't seen Megan yet.

181

"Mum?" Megan called, hurrying over to the van. "What are you doing here?"

To her amazement, her mother grabbed her, threw both arms around her and hugged her so hard, Megan couldn't catch her breath. "You're all right, oh, thank goodness!" Adrienne babbled.

Megan could feel her mother's body shaking. "Mum, what's wrong?"

Adrienne pulled away then, looked into Megan's face. She seemed to be drinking it in, as if she couldn't believe it was real. "I saw that ambulance and I thought . . . I don't know what I thought, but it wasn't good. You sure you're OK?"

"Yes, I'm fine." She couldn't tell her mother just yet what had happened. That would have to wait until they got home. "What are you doing here? I told you Dan was bringing me home."

"I thought *I* was taking you home," Jade said petulantly. "Weren't we going out for pizza?"

Megan had forgotten. She *had* made plans to do just that with her friends following the meeting. But that had been last Tuesday, thousands of years ago, before the picnic, before Leah, before the rubbish bin, before Dan.

"Megan," her mother said, her voice trembling, "the police were at the house. Just now. Two officers. They said the milk you gave the cat was poisoned. Poisoned, Megan! Some kind

182

of deadly insecticide. And it was in *our* fridge in *our* shop. Megan, practically everyone in town knows I'm severely allergic to milk. I've made jokes about it in the shop, remember? Lots of people know."

"Mum. . ."

Her mother put a hand up. "So the police are certain that poison was meant only for you. For *you*, Megan! That's why I got so hysterical when I saw the ambulance pulling away just now. I thought you . . . you . . . Megan, I am trying to tell you that someone tried to poison you!"

Twenty-Two

The two police officers, one of whom was Dan's brother Eddie, were waiting when Megan's mother brought her, along with Dan, Jade, and Joseph, back to the house. When a still-shaken Adrienne had made coffee and brought a tray into the pretty blue-and-white living room, questions were posed to Megan. Questions she couldn't have answered even if her mind hadn't been foggy with shock and disbelief.

Did she know why anyone would want to harm her? Poison her?

No, she didn't.

The poison used was a strong insecticide. Did she know anyone who gardened? "No, but my mother does," Megan said through lips that felt numb.

Adrienne, sitting between Megan and Dan on the blue striped couch, sent her a questioning look. "I do?"

"The silent partners. I thought you said they all belonged

to the Glenview Garden Club. Zoe's mother grows great roses, you said, and Beth's mother's speciality is chrysanthemums, and Lily's mother has the best gardener in town, right?"

"Oh. Them. Yes, that's true. I thought you meant friends of mine. None of my friends have time to garden. But yes, the partners do have beautiful gardens." Adrienne pointed to a lush spring bouquet of yellow, blue, and white flowers sitting on the coffee table. "They often bring flowers into the shop. I keep them there a few days, and then bring them home to enjoy them." She smiled wanly at Jade. "And your mother grows lovely flowers."

"Yeah, she does. But I don't think she uses insecticide. I think she does that organic thing."

"Could you give me the names of these people?" Officer McGill asked, pencil poised over his notebook.

The other officer said, "I know their names. Except that last one. Her name was?"

Jade's flush deepened. Megan knew why. It was as if he had said the other three women were well-known, but her own mother wasn't anybody important.

The partners, Megan thought cynically, must donate some of their shedloads of money to the Policemen's Benevolent Fund. She hoped that didn't mean they'd get special treatment. Not that she thought any of them had tossed her into a giant rubbish bin. She almost laughed out loud then, at the vision of the chic, well-coiffed women lurking around in the alley.

It wasn't funny, though, was it? *Someone* had been lurking in the alley, expecting Megan to drink that poisoned milk and die. Die! When the cat had died instead, the plan had to be changed, so she'd been thrown into the bin and it had been set on fire. Someone had tried to kill her.

"Who else has access to the shop? I mean, who has keys?" an officer asked Adrienne.

"Let me see." She began ticking off on her fingers. "I do, of course, and my daughter. I keep several extras around, here at the house and at the shop, just in case. I'm not one to lose things, but you never know. Then there are the partners. Each of them has a key, although as far as I know they've never used them."

"I have one," Jade said, "because I work there. And sometimes I lend it to Joseph if he has an early pick-up or delivery."

"You do?" Adrienne looked surprised. "I didn't know that. I really don't want you lending the key to anyone, Jade. Not even Joseph. If he has an early delivery, I'll be at the shop to let him in."

Unperturbed, Joseph nodded, but Jade lowered her eyes in shame. "Sorry," she murmured.

"Anyone else?" McGill asked.

"No. I think that's it."

"Mum," Megan felt compelled to point out, "the key ring hangs right beside the cash register. You said yourself you keep extras. Do you count them every night to make sure they're all still there?"

Doubt appeared in her mother's face. "Well, no, not *every* night. But. . ."

"The shop's been really crowded lately, Mum. Like a zoo. Anyone could have slipped one of those keys off the ring while we were busy away from the register."

"But I do count the keys," Adrienne protested; "Not every single night, maybe, but often enough. I counted them this morning. They're all there."

The older officer's voice was noncommittal as he said, "Someone could have made a copy. Slip the key off the ring, take it to a locksmith and have a copy made, bring it right back, slip it back on the ring. Wouldn't take more than a few minutes."

Adrienne was very pale. "And that's how you think someone managed to slip the poison into the milk carton?"

"Not necessarily. I've been in your shop. It's small, with easy access to the back rooms and that room upstairs. Could be, when you were busy like your daughter says, someone walked right into that back room with the fridge, opened it up, dumped the insecticide in the milk and walked back out again. Someone who was already inside the shop."

"Maybe," Megan said. "But they couldn't have stolen Leah's dress, the one my mother was working on, while we were in the shop. We'd have noticed them leaving with it. So, since there wasn't any broken lock after that dress was missing, they must have used a key."

She hadn't realized until she saw the puzzled look on the officers' faces that her mother had failed to report the stolen dress. An explanation was required. Adrienne handled it. "I didn't report it," she finished, "because the dress wasn't expensive enough to make it grand theft. With everything else that was going on, I didn't think petty theft was worth the attention. Should I have reported it?"

"Only because it might be part of the whole picture, ma'am," Officer McGill said.

"I think it is," Megan said firmly. "And I don't think the attack on Lily had anything to do with the money. It's got something to do with the prom."

She was instantly sorry. The officers looked uninterested, but Adrienne bolted upright on the sofa, alarm on her face. Megan could practically see the images in her mother's mind: an explosion at the gym the night of the prom, a fire, mass murder . . .

"But maybe not," Megan added hastily. If Adrienne

became convinced that the insane acts were related to the prom, even she, who had ardently wanted her daughter to go, might change her mind and make that daughter stay at home. "I'm sure," Megan added weakly, "that the poisoning attempt has nothing to do with the prom at all. That's too silly. How could it?"

The officers stood up. "We need to find out where that insecticide came from," one of them said. "When we know that, we'll be able to give you some answers. In the meantime, we're still working on that girl's death out at the Point." He looked at Megan. "Lucky that milk carton and saucer survived the fire, or we wouldn't even know this thing had happened. You'd be out there without a parachute, miss, like that other girl, the one who died, not knowing someone had it in for you. At least you've had some warning. You take care now, you hear? We'll get back to you as soon as we know something."

Does it really matter, Megan wondered wearily as her mother led the officers to the door, *why* this is happening? Even if the prom isn't involved, Leah will still be dead, Lily will still have a face that looks like she fell from a twelve-storey building onto cement, and I will still be scared half out of my wits. Correction, *completely* out of my wits.

Jade and Joseph left, but Dan hung around all evening. Megan could see that he was reluctant to leave her, even if she was safe in her own home. His obvious concern warmed her like a wool jumper.

"You *have* to go home," she said shortly after eleven. They were sitting on the porch swing. The temperature hadn't dropped, and the motion of the swing provided them with a balmy breeze. A three-quarter moon overhead acted as a faint lamp. Adrienne had tactfully withdrawn to her own room, but Megan knew she probably wasn't asleep. "We've got school tomorrow. I don't want you dragging into your classes with bags under your eyes."

"Why not?" His worried look was momentarily replaced by the hint of a grin. "I've already got a date for the prom, so I figure I can slack off now. Are you so shallow that you'd break a date with me just because I'm not my usual drop-dead, gorgeous self?"

Megan didn't laugh. "Please don't mention the prom," she said softly, leaning back against his chest.

"Sorry." His arm tightened round her shoulders. "Are you going to be OK? Look at me, Meg."

She turned her head, and he repeated, "You're going to be OK, right?"

She couldn't very well say, No, I'm not. She said yes. "Yes, I'm going to be just fine," was what she said. But her mind was not at all convinced.

Before he left, he said, "Look, everyone knows about that

bin business. So people will be watching out for you. Not just me, lots of people. You won't be alone, I promise. I'll pick you up and take you to school, and bring you home afterwards, or to the shop if that's where you want to go."

"Jade picks me up every morning."

"I'm bigger than Jade," and now he really did grin. "She won't mind. She'll want you to be safe, right?"

Megan wasn't so sure Jade wouldn't mind. But the truth was, she *would* feel safer with Dan. Maybe that was sexist, but she couldn't help it.

She would have to call Jade later. It probably wouldn't be a great conversation.

"And Eddie knows how I feel about you," Dan said after he kissed her goodnight, "so he won't let anyone ease up on this case, OK?"

Those were the words that finally carried Megan off to sleep in the small hours of the morning. "*Eddie knows how I feel about you.*"

Jade hadn't been angry when Megan called. She had said she understood, and was glad Megan had Dan "watching out" for her. But then she had added wistfully, "I wish I had someone like that."

Megan had wanted to tell her that her mother was saving the turquoise dress for her, but she didn't. Jade had to ask Joseph because she wanted to go with him, not because she

191

wanted to wear a particular dress. That wouldn't be fair to Joseph.

School was grim. Exams were racing towards them. Everyone knew they should be concentrating like mad. Impossible. Normal anxiety about grades had been compounded by a very real fear of physical danger. It was in countless faces as Megan walked through the hallways, always with Dan or Jade, Joseph or Lucy or Sophie at her side. She saw it everywhere. Fear. Atmos*fear,* she thought, realizing that the looks sent her way contained some measure of awe because she'd survived an attack and wasn't even in hospital. But what she also saw in those faces as they passed her was a wariness, a knowledge that she might very well be the target of an additional attack. Unless they were willing to risk being caught in the crossfire, they'd be wise to steer clear of Megan Dunne.

It was weird. Four years of high school almost over and only now, in the last two weeks, did everyone know who she was.

I would rather still be anonymous, she thought, and knew that it was true.

She learned via the school grapevine that Lily hadn't been able to identify her attacker. Couldn't even tell if it was a guy or a girl. The words that had been whispered in her ear had been repeated so many times around school that they had become an exaggerated version of the truth, including a bizarre threat to "cut off her toes and post them to her in a box if she went to the prom".

Of course she wasn't going. That word, too, circulated very quickly. Lily had tearfully broken her date with David. She was terrified, and even if she hadn't been, everyone who knew her knew she wouldn't appear in public until her face was completely back to normal.

Handsome, popular David Goumas, like Michael Danz before him, no longer had a date for his senior prom. But this time, Megan's friends were careful not to rejoice while she was present. When Lucy asked her at lunch if there were any prom dresses left at the shop, she did it so casually, almost lazily, that Megan refused to make an issue of it. "Yes. About ten, I think." She did not mention David Goumas.

And later, when she spied Jade and Lucy talking sympathetically to a despondent David, Megan kept right on walking with Dan. She wasn't about to say to her friends: "Be careful what you wish for. If I were you, I wouldn't be so anxious for a prom date now. Look what's been happening to those of us who *are* going." Because even if she could be absolutely positive that *was* the reason behind the attacks, she knew they wouldn't listen. No matter what, they'd still want to go. They wouldn't believe that something as awful as the attacks could happen to them. Impossible to believe until you actually feared for your life, as she had. If someone had told Megan Dunne that accepting Dan McGill's invitation meant that someone would try to poison her, would she still have accepted? Or would she have said no?

If I had really believed it, she told herself, I would have said no. I'm no masochist. The trouble is, I wouldn't have believed it. It would have sounded totally insane.

It still did.

There was no announcement that the prom was being cancelled. Leah's mother replaced the missing funds, accompanying the cheque with a note that said her daughter would have wanted her to, and generously wishing everyone a good time.

When Dan dropped Megan off at Quartet shortly after three, Adrienne was waiting at the door for her. Her face was strained, her mouth pursed in an anxious line.

It must have been hard for her all day, Megan thought, giving her mother a hug. I should have called her more than that once at lunchtime. Tomorrow I will.

But in the next moment, she learned that it wasn't only her safety that had her mother upset.

"Megan, it's happened again," Adrienne said in a low voice to avoid being overheard by a handful of customers in the shop, which included a few Pops and, Megan saw, Lucy and Sophie, browsing among the remaining prom dresses.

Megan's initial reaction was that her mother meant there had been another attack. Her heart began racing. "Oh, no! Who is it this time?"

Adrienne shook her head. "No, no, not that. No one's been hurt. But another dress is missing. One of those three I had to replace? It's not here. Like the other one, it was finished, hanging by the register, and ready to be picked up, although I hadn't called and told her yet. But it's gone."

Confused, Megan said, "No, that can't be right. Leah's dress disappeared after she was . . . killed. Like her attacker was sending a message or something. Lily Pappas is the girl who was attacked at school yesterday, so it would be *her* dress that's missing. But . . . Lily didn't buy her dress here, Mum. She went to the city, just like she always does. So how could her dress be missing?"

"I know Lily didn't buy her prom dress here, Megan. I'm not talking about her. But one of the dresses *is* missing. It's the blue one. That pale blue slip dress. The one Beth Andrews bought. It's gone. It's simply gone. I can't find it anywhere."

"Beth? Beth's dress is missing?"

Adrienne fixed apprehensive eyes on Megan. "I don't like this, Megan. I don't like it at all. That girl could be in serious danger."

Twenty-Three

"Maybe Beth came in and got the dress, Mum," Megan suggested. "When you were at lunch?"

"I didn't go to lunch today. I never left the shop. And there's something else." Adrienne pointed to a vase of flowers sitting on the counter. "Lily's mother brought those in today. I asked her if she uses insecticide, and she said of course, but it was the oddest thing, she'd had a brand-new bottle in her garage and when she went out to garden today, the bottle had gone. She said the last time she noticed that it was there was the day of Leah's funeral, when Beth's boyfriend came over to pick up small bouquets of flowers she'd put together for Leah's friends to carry. She and the boy went into the garage to find a small box to put them in. She said the insecticide was there then."

"Jordan? She thinks Jordan took the insecticide?"

"She didn't say that, Megan. But they keep their garage

196

locked. If he was the only one in there . . . I'm calling the police. Beth could be in danger."

Of *course* Beth is in danger, Megan thought. Aren't we all? She kept the thought to herself. "It's weird that *my* dress wasn't stolen." Or. . . "It wasn't, was it?" she asked nervously.

"Your dress isn't here. I took it home with me, so no one would buy it."

"Good thinking. Thanks." Megan barely knew Jordan. Why would he try to poison her? But he was a big guy. He could easily have lifted her into that bin.

As Adrienne went to phone the police, the door flew open and Jade breezed in. She seemed surprised to find Megan standing just inside the entrance. Her face fell. "Now what?"

Megan told her about the dress.

"I don't see what's so scary about that," Jade said. "A missing dress? We already know whoever is doing this doesn't want his victims to attend the prom, right? In Beth's case, he must have thought another act of violence was too risky, with every police officer in town looking for him. So he just took the dress. You should be relieved, not worried."

Scepticism moved Megan to say, "Jade, everyone who knows Beth knows she can afford to buy another dress in plenty of time for the prom. Stealing the one she already bought isn't going to keep her at home." Then she repeated what Adrienne had told her about the insecticide in Lily's garage.

197

"Jordan?" Jade asked sceptically. "That's crazy. Why would Jordan poison you? He doesn't even know you."

"I know it's crazy," Megan said pointedly. "Doesn't that tell you something? Look, Joseph's got the van. Will you take me to find Beth? We should warn her. Don't tell my mother. She'll never let us go. I'll tell her we have errands to run for the prom. She'll let me go if I don't go alone."

Adrienne returned to say that she had called Beth's house first. "She had a hair appointment this afternoon," Adrienne said. "The housekeeper didn't know where, but the officer I spoke to then said he'd find out. There's nothing more we can do now."

Oh, yeah, there is, Megan thought. We can find Beth ourselves, and tell her what's going on.

She told Adrienne they had errands to run, and although her mother expressed reservations about Megan leaving the shop, she finally gave in. "Come back here the minute you're done, OK? And be careful, Megan. You and Jade stay together the whole time, promise?"

Megan promised. While Jade ran to the ladies to adjust an irritating contact lens, Megan limped upstairs to deposit her books and jumper in the Sweatbox. After one more anxious warning from Adrienne to be careful, they left the shop.

In the car, Jade asked, "So Beth's having her hair done. Any idea where?"

"Probably the most expensive, classiest place in town."

"That would be on the East Side," Jade said. "Out there by Glenview Hills, where all the Pops live. I'm game if you are." She grinned. "Although the air will probably be much more rarified there than it is down here. Maybe we should take oxygen masks. I still think you're overreacting. It's not like Beth was actually attacked."

Not yet, Megan thought.

"This is kind of fun," Jade said cheerfully as she expertly wove her car through traffic towards the East Side of Glenview. "Like being on a treasure hunt. Or, we could pretend we're detectives, looking for a missing witness, right? We used to do silly stuff like that all the time, Megan. Remember? And when we went out to the Point, we pretended we were members of an international secret organization. You and Sophie and Lucy and I."

"We were little kids then, Jade, and besides, we were never in any real danger." Megan's knee was throbbing, and her head ached. She had no idea what they were going to say when they found Beth. We just came to inform you that someone stole your prom dress and my mother thinks that means something ominous and she also thinks you shouldn't get too cozy with your boyfriend right now? What was Beth supposed to do about all that? No point in buying a new dress, since she might not be going with Jordan, after all. If Jordan *had* stolen that insecticide and dumped it into a carton of milk at Quartet, Jordan wouldn't be going to the prom.

And so Beth wouldn't go, and then Beth wouldn't be queen, which was what she wanted more than anything. The drawing proved that. Megan's mind raced. Just how much did Jordan love Beth? Enough to erase all of the competition for something that Beth really wanted?

But *I'm* no competition for Beth, Megan reminded herself sternly. Unless Jordan believed that if she went with Dan, she might stand a chance simply because Dan was so popular. Was that possible?

But if she *was* right, Beth was the one girl in Glenview who didn't have to worry. Jordan was trying to protect her, not hurt her. Still, she had a right to know what was going on.

Why would Jordan have stolen her prom dress?

"This is so stupid!" Megan cried heatedly, startling Jade, who jumped. "I cannot believe that someone is attacking girls to keep them from attending their senior prom! It's so totally insane! I just don't get it."

"I do." The late afternoon sun was hitting the windscreen. Jade pulled the visor on her side into place to shield her eyes. "I kind of know how they feel."

"Oh, Jade, that's ridiculous! You do *not*! You've never hurt another person in your *life*!"

"You haven't known me my whole life. Only since fifth grade. Anyway, I didn't say I agreed with what he or she is doing. But it's obviously someone who isn't going to the dance, hasn't been invited, and is angry about it. And that I *do* understand. You should, too. God knows we've sat out enough formal dances."

Although Megan's new theory was very different from Jade's, she didn't say so. She could be totally wrong about Jordan. "Yes, but we never felt like killing anyone, did we?"

Jade's half smile was impossible to read. "No, I guess not. Might have thought about it once or twice, though. Didn't you?"

"No. Do you really think we know someone who is so insane they did *more* than just think about it?"

"Sure." Jade whipped the car round a sharp corner. "Maybe even more than one person. It's just not the kind of insanity that's obvious, that's all. We studied people like that in psychology class, remember? The kind who keep their illness hidden. They're very clever. No one ever knows how ill they are until something horrible happens. Like now. Because the rest of the time, the signs aren't right out there in front of us. We all have these weird ideas about insanity, images of screaming, shrieking people running around in the streets. It's hardly ever really like that. It's a lot more subtle, especially with someone who kills people."

"What makes you such an expert?" Megan was thinking that Jade's description *could* fit Jordan. He seemed normal enough.

"I've read a lot about it. The subject interests me, and as you know, I have a lot of time on my hands to read. And we *do* know people like that, Megan. I'll bet we'd be really surprised to find out who they are. Probably the people we would least suspect. Lily, frankly, always struck me as teetering on the edge. She was trying too hard. Zoe, too, and Beth never quite measured up to the others, so that could have driven her over the edge."

Jade screeched to a halt in front of a small, upmarket shopping centre, set some distance back from the street and beautifully landscaped with neatly-trimmed spring flower beds. A sign in hot pink hanging in front of one of the low, white buildings read *Shear Delight*. "You just never know about people, Megan. You *think* you know them, but you don't. Not really."

While Megan dealt with that depressing thought, they climbed out of the car into bright sunshine.

"Did you know that David's taking a cousin of his to the prom?" Megan asked as they hurried to the salon entrance. "She's only a sophomore. Lily set it up. She didn't want David to miss his prom. I think that's kind of nice, don't you? That she cared enough to make him go even though she couldn't?"

"Adorable." Jade opened the salon door. "*He* wasn't available for very long! Lucy's crushed. So is every other girl at school who doesn't have a date yet."

"I'm sure."

Beth wasn't in the salon, and they were told that no one by that name had an appointment.

Back in the car, they hit three more salons in East Glenview. Megan's anxiety increased when they didn't find Beth in any of them. Had the police taken her mother's call seriously? Were they looking for Beth, too? And maybe Jordan as well?

"This isn't fun any more," Jade commented as they drove through the streets of East Glenview. "We'll try one more, and then that's it. I'm tired. There's a place a couple of streets up that's really posh. Let's hope she's in there."

"This was *never* fun," Megan retorted. "We're not looking for Beth to invite her to a sleepover, Jade. We're looking for her to give her bad news. How could that possibly be fun?"

"Well, you know what I mean. It's kind of fun for the two of us to be doing something together. Like we used to. Graduation is scaring me a bit, Megan. I mean, I know we're both going to uni together, but I have this awful feeling that things will be really different at college." Jade turned a corner. "Anyway, I know Dan is going there, too, so you'll probably be spending tons of time with him and will forget about all your old friends. We said that would never happen, but all kids say that. Then they grow up and it happens." There was no cheerfulness left in her voice as she added, "I just have this awful feeling about everything changing."

"It could change in a good way," Megan said, and at the same moment, spotted Beth, with a new haircut, walking to her car, parked at the curb directly in front of them. "There she is!" she shrieked. "There's Beth!"

Then everything happened at once. And even though Megan knew it had to have happened quickly, in a matter of seconds, it seemed to her to have taken place in slow motion.

Beth climbed into her car.

Jade slammed on the brake.

Her car squealed to a halt.

But not in time.

It crashed with a resounding clang of metal on metal into the back of Beth's new graduation present, a shiny black VW Golf.

The impact popped Beth's boot open.

People coming out of the shopping centre came to a standstill. People driving by on the tree-lined side street slowed down. Some cars came to a halt. A woman coming out of the salon whirled round and ran back inside to phone for help.

"Oh, no, oh, no," Jade moaned as her own car shuddered

to a halt, "I don't have my contacts in. They were driving me nuts so I took them out at the shop and it says on my licence, *Must wear corrective lenses*. Oh, no, I am going to be in such trouble for this!" Unbloodied and unbruised thanks to her safety belt, Jade turned to Megan, desperation in her eyes. "Megan, please, if you've ever been my friend for even one second, be my friend now! Do not, please, do not mention to the police officer who will surely be here any second now, that I am not wearing my contacts, OK? Please, Megan! I'm in enough trouble as it is. My dad is going to have seven fits!"

Shaken but uninjured, Megan asked, "Won't a police officer be able to tell that you don't have your lenses in?"

"No, of course not. Just don't say anything, OK?" Jade's hands were shaking visibly. "We'd better go and face the music." She uttered a short, bitter laugh. "And you thought we were *already* bringing her bad news, right?"

Eddie McGill pulled up. He was alone. His window down, he glanced at the driver of the damaged car and called as the two girls slowly emerged from their own car, "Driver's fine. Bumped her head, that's all, looks like. Be right with you," and he pulled the car over to the curb across the street.

"I am a dead person," Jade muttered as Beth pushed open the driver's door and slowly, carefully climbed out, one hand to her forehead. "I won't be allowed to drive again until I'm seventy-five years old."

Beth, still holding her head, walked dazedly around to the rear of her car, staring at the damage in horrified dismay.

"Beth," Jade stammered, "I'm sorry, I'm so sorry, the sun was in my eyes and I didn't realize how close we were. Our insurance will pay for the damage. I am really sorry."

Beth moved then, took a step, then another towards the rear of her car, just as Officer McGill arrived. "I see you found her for me," he said to Megan and Jade. "I got a call to keep an eye out for this car. I didn't quite expect to find it in this shape, though."

"I should close that boot," Beth said, her voice emotionless. "I should go and do that."

Megan was standing directly to the right of the open lid. "It probably won't close," she said, "but I'll give it a shot." She put a hand on the lid and would have tried to shove it closed if she hadn't seen the contents. What she saw inside the boot brought a gasp of disbelief.

Hearing the gasp, McGill moved to join Megan behind the car. "What?"

Megan said nothing. But her eyes never left the interior of the boot.

"Well, well, well," Dan's brother said slowly. "What have we here?" He reached into the boot to lift out and display in front of Beth and Jade a beautiful red dress with spaghetti straps and a short, full skirt. He handed the dress to Megan, who took it, and then his hands went into the depths of the trunk again. A pale blue dress, as slender and delicate as a flower.

Beth's dress.

She stole it herself? Megan thought, her eyes on Officer McGill's hands. Why would she do that? And what is she doing with Leah's dress?

The hands dipped into the boot again. This time when they came out, the dress was black. Zoe's. Adrienne must not have noticed yet that it, too, was missing, or she would have said something.

Megan was now holding all three dresses. When the officer reached into the boot again, the item he brought out was much smaller. A headband in a vivid yellow print. "That's Leah's!" Megan cried. "Leah Markham's. She was wearing it the day of the picnic. We all thought it came off and blew out to sea when she fell, but there it is! And," waving the clothing in her arms, "this red dress is the prom dress my mother told you about. It was stolen from the shop, remember? All three of these dresses are from the shop and here they are, in. . ." Megan looked up at Beth standing beside the boot, her face bone-white ". . .in Beth's boot," she finished lamely.

"What else is in there?" Jade asked, coming up behind Megan.

"Well, there's this," the officer said, holding up a large plastic bottle with a red label. "Insecticide." He turned to Beth. "Now why would someone be carrying a bottle of insecticide around in their car boot, unless they're in the gardening business. Which I don't think you are, miss, am I right?"

"I. . . I. . ." Beth looked ill.

"And here," Eddie McGill said, replacing the insecticide bottle and reaching into the boot again, "we have what I suspect might be the money missing from Glenview High School." This time, he held up a grey metal box, clearly labelled on the top: *Prom.*

But he dropped it back into the boot in time to catch Beth as her eyes closed and her knees folded like paper money, and she collapsed.

The officer caught her before she hit the ground.

208

Twenty-Four

"I don't see why you're so bent out of shape about this," Jade said on the way home. Beth, who had regained consciousness once only to immediately faint again, had been taken to hospital under police guard. "Didn't I tell you it would be someone we'd least suspect? Beth was the nicest of the Pops, so we should have guessed it was her."

Megan remembered Beth asking her in hospital if she had seen the person who had attacked her. Probably afraid that I could identify her, Megan thought numbly. She told Jade about the drawing. "I can't believe she wanted to be queen that much. Enough to kill. And me? She thought I was competition?"

"Because you're going with Dan. He's a popular guy. Besides," Jade added matter-of-factly, "by the time Adrienne works her magic on you, you'll be the prettiest girl at that dance."

"Where on earth have you been?" Adrienne greeted Megan worriedly as she entered the shop. Jade had the rest of the afternoon off. She had dropped off Megan, promising to call later, and driven away. "I've been frantic. I didn't expect you to be gone so long. The police just called. They've found Beth. It's all over, Megan." Relief coated Adrienne's words, and her normal colour had returned. "That poor child is responsible for the horrible things that have been going on in town. Her mother must just be distraught."

Megan explained, to Adrienne's horror, her involvement in Beth's being taken away for questioning. "I thought it was Jordan," she admitted. "It's hard to believe Beth is strong enough to toss me into that bin."

Adrienne looked unhappy. Of all the silent partners, she liked Beth's mother best. "Strength of a madman, I guess. Isn't that what they say? On the other hand, Megan, we don't have any real proof that Beth did those things. Maybe she didn't. We should wait and see."

"Mu-um! I saw the stuff in her boot! It was all there. Car boots lock automatically. You need a key to open them. Beth had a key. End of story."

"They didn't take her to the police station," Adrienne said, locking the front door and turning the sign to read *Closed*. "She's in hospital right now, under police guard. She'll stay there until they know she's all right." She moved to the back of the shop, to the cash register. "Is that why you were gone so long? Because of the accident?"

Megan confessed then, that they hadn't gone to run errands. That they'd left the shop to look for Beth. "It took us forever to find the right salon."

Adrienne looked up from the register, a puzzled crease furrowing her brow. "I don't understand. Jade knew where Beth was. I told her."

Megan leaned against the counter, facing her mother. "No, you didn't. Remember, you didn't know. You said you called the house—"

Adrienne interrupted her. "That was the first time I called. The housekeeper answered. But after you went upstairs, I called again, and this time Beth's mother answered. I didn't tell her why I was calling, because I didn't want to alarm her. I simply said that you needed to see Beth about something, and she told me where Beth was. Then I went to the ladies and told Jade. I wanted you to know that Beth had been located. I thought it would set your mind at rest. The door was half open, so I called out the name of the salon. I know she heard me, because she said, 'OK, thanks.' She was putting her contacts in. Then I called the police again and gave them the name of the salon."

"You mean she was taking them *out*." Jade had known all

along where Beth was? Then why had they gone on that stupid wild goose chase all over East Glenview?

"No. She was putting them *in*. I have contacts myself, Megan. I know the difference between putting them in and taking them out. Jade was definitely putting hers in. I know she has trouble with them. I just assumed she'd taken them out to rinse them, maybe to make sure they'd be OK while she was driving."

"But she said. . ."

"Megan, what's the matter? You have a very strange look on your face."

"Nothing." Megan's mind reeled dizzily. She had to think. Impossible to think now. Too bewildered. Why would Jade lie? "Is Joseph working today?"

"No. I didn't need him. Why?"

"I need to talk to him. I'll go up to the Sweatbox and call him. Are you leaving now?"

"No, you and I are leaving together tonight. Maybe Beth did those things and maybe she didn't, but I'm not taking any chances. I'll take you home and then meet Sam at the restaurant. As soon as you've called Joseph, we'll go."

Good thinking, Megan thought heavily as she hurried up the narrow staircase. Better to be safe than sorry. Especially since, after what her mother had told her, there was a chance that Beth was as innocent as a newborn baby.

Jade had lied. She had known the name of the salon all along, and she *was* wearing her contacts. Had she hit Beth's car on purpose? Did she already know what was in the boot? Had she guessed correctly that slamming into the Golf would open the lid? She had to know the accident would bring the police. And they would see the evidence in the boot. Then Beth would be taken away.

There was only one way Jade could possibly have known what was inside Beth Andrews' trunk. She could only have known if she had put the things there herself.

Megan had no idea how Jade could have done that. Stolen Beth's keys, maybe, made copies, and then returned them.

The depressing truth was, it made far more sense that the attacker be someone like Jade, who had never been invited to a prom, including this one, than someone like Beth, who only wanted to be queen.

Megan dialled Joseph's number. How could your best friend be completely insane without you knowing it? But Jade herself had explained that, hadn't she? *"The people you would least suspect"*, she had said.

Joseph answered. "The night the dresses were stolen and destroyed," she said bluntly. "What time did Jade get to the library?"

The answer he gave was not the one she wanted to hear. "We were supposed to study together. But Jade didn't get

213

there until ten or fifteen minutes before the library closed. Then you showed up. Luckily, I'd done enough studying before she got there."

"She didn't get there until right before the library closed?"

"Nope. Said she had to go home and take her contacts out. Couldn't study with them in. Had to get her glasses."

The contacts again. So convenient. "Was she wearing her glasses when she got there?"

"Yeah, I think so. If she hadn't been, I would have said something about it. I was annoyed that she was so late. So I think she was. Why?"

Megan couldn't tell him. He'd find out soon enough anyway, and he'd be crushed. The girl he adored. Who might be very ill. If nothing else, she'd been lying like crazy lately. Crazy . . . was Jade really insane? Was that why she'd been doing so much reading about mental illness, because she was afraid she had it? *"People you would least suspect."* Well, that certainly included Jade.

Jade had been moved around a lot as a child. For the first nine years, she had never stayed in one place for more than a year. She had never made any friends, she had no roots, no stability in her life until she'd moved to Glenview and met Sophie and Lucy and Megan. Could all that instability make someone mentally ill? And could they really hide it all that time?

So disturbed by her thoughts that her hands and knees were shaking, Megan went back downstairs. "Why don't you go ahead and meet Sam?" she said to her mother. "I'll close. Like you said, Beth's safely in hospital, under police guard. Nothing can happen tonight. And –" grabbing at the first garment she saw, which happened to be pink, a colour she loathed – "I want to wear this shirt, but I'll need to iron it. I'll do it upstairs, so I can change before Dan gets here. Go on. I'll be fine, I promise." She needed to be alone, to think.

"You hate pink." Her mother peered over the cash register at her. "Megan, has something else happened? Something I don't know about? You *would* tell me, wouldn't you?"

"Of course I would. I think it's all catching up with me, that's all. I need to get out with Dan and have some fun, and I need this shirt, too. So, can I close?"

Adrienne hesitated. "Isn't Dan picking you up at the house? I told you to tell him I wasn't leaving you here alone tonight, that he should go there instead of here."

"I'll call him and tell him there's been a change of plan."

"Fine. But I'm calling the hospital first to make sure Beth is still under police guard." Which she did. She nodded as she hung up. "She is. I guess that means the police still think she's the one. She must be very, very ill. Well, all right then, sweetheart, I guess you can lock up. If you're sure. . ."

"Really, Mum, it'll be fine. Now, I've got to go and iron

this shirt. I'll pay for it on payday, OK? Here are the tags." If her mother noticed Megan's trembling hands as she placed the tags on the counter, she said nothing.

"All right," Adrienne said with some reluctance. "But I'll just be across the alley at the restaurant if you need anything, anything at all. Megan?"

But Megan was already on her way upstairs.

Her mother came to the foot of the stairs just once, to call goodbye. "You be sure to call Dan, OK, and tell him you're here?"

"Right. Have fun!" But Megan had no intention of calling Dan. Not yet. She began ironing the pink shirt.

As soon as she heard the door slam after her mother, she put the iron down on the ironing board and went to the telephone.

She sank into a leather chair beside the open window and, with trembling hands, dialled Jade LaSalle's number.

Twenty-Five

*S*tupid Michael, going off to Utah. Stupid David, taking some dumb old cousin, when he could have taken me. And Beth's mother informed me when I called the hospital, pretending that I didn't know everyone in town considers her daughter a homicidal maniac, that Jordan won't be going to the prom at all. I slid that question in there so subtly, so cleverly, she didn't even seem aware that asking was totally tasteless. He is not going. Not without Beth. Idiot. I am not going to ask him just so I can be told no. I should have known.

That only leaves Dan. He's the best one, anyway.

All I have to do is get Megan out of the way.

What do I do about Beth? If I finish off Megan while Beth is under police guard, they'll know Beth couldn't have done it. Then it will all have been a waste of time. Meeting her at the mall to pick up the prom candles, offering to take the boxes out to her car, borrowing her car keys, then moving the dresses and

217

all that other stuff from my boot to hers, planning it so carefully. All of it for nothing.

It's hilarious, when you stop and think about it; I made that anonymous call to the police, telling them to search Beth's car, and then bang! the accident happens and the boot pops open and that officer comes along just in time to see a boot full of incriminating evidence. Perfect! A sign that all of this was meant to be.

Anyway, when this is over and I'm dancing in Dan's arms, someone else has to take the rap, and Beth is perfect. At this point, I think she's not even sure she didn't kill Leah. Beth is so easily rattled.

I haven't felt this good since the night I sneaked up that fire escape and did a number on those stupid prom dresses. Driving over them felt so satisfying. I think that's when I made up my mind that I would go, no matter what. But it wasn't until Leah died that I figured out how.

Stealing the replacement dresses was a piece of cake. Nice of Adrienne to leave a key ring right there by the cash register. No one even noticed they were gone when I slipped them into my jacket pocket and ran down the street to have copies made. Put them right back, easy as pie, a few minutes later. Then I could go in and out of the shop any time I wanted. Still can.

We took an oath, the four of us. We were supposed to stick together, that's what we promised each other. We always spent prom night together. But that wasn't going to happen this year, was it? Megan was going to ruin the whole thing. Every other year it happened the way it was supposed to. But not this year.

I know it can never be the same again. I've accepted that. Even with Megan out of the picture, it's too late now. It won't be the same.

But at least I'll have what I want. And wasn't that the goal all along?

I will have to take Beth with me when I deal with Megan. No choice there.

How am I going to get rid of the cop guarding her?

I'll think of something.

Nothing's going to stop me now.

Twenty-Six

"Because, Megan," Jade said in answer to Megan's question about why they had driven all over the place that afternoon when Jade knew where Beth was all along, "it was nice to be doing something with you for a change. I know it was stupid. But it felt so much like the kind of stuff we used to do, I didn't want it to end. So I stretched it out a little, that's all. Is that such a crime?"

Was it? Maybe it was just one *part* of a crime? "You said you didn't have your contacts in. You said that was why you hit Beth's car, Jade. But Mum said she saw you putting them in at the shop."

Jade sighed with what sounded like impatience. "I never said I hit the car because I didn't have my contacts in, Megan. I said the police would fine me if they knew I didn't have them in. Because it says on my licence that I need them. I hit Beth's car because you shrieked at me and I panicked and misjudged the distance between her car and mine. I *didn't* have them in. Why would I lie about that?"

"But Mum said—"

"Your mother's right," Jade interrupted. "When she saw me in the ladies, I *was* putting them in. But they started driving me crazy again, so I took them right back out. In fact, they're sitting on the sink at the shop because I forgot to stick them in my bag. They should still be there. If I'd had them with me, Megan, I'd have put them in before that police officer turned up." Jade's voice cooled. "If you're at the shop, go and look in the ladies."

Megan didn't need to. She knew Jade was telling the truth. The accident had been just that, nothing more. And Jade LaSalle wasn't any more insane than Megan Dunne was.

"What I want to know," Jade continued, "is what's going on here? Why the third degree? You didn't find *my* boot full of souvenirs, did you?" When Megan remained mute, squirming uncomfortably in her chair, Jade said softly, "Oh, Megan. This doesn't mean what I think it means, does it? You thought that I. . ."

"No, no," Megan said hastily, feeling her cheeks burning. "Not really. I know you'd never hurt me, Jade. It was just . . . well, Mum said you knew about the salon, and she said you had your contacts in, and none of it made sense, so I just thought I'd call and find out, that's all."

"Are you at the shop?" Jade asked sharply.

"Yes."

"I'm coming over there. Do *not* go anywhere!" Click.

Oh, man, Megan thought despondently, how am I ever going to make this up to her? She knows I suspected her. She's never going to forgive me.

Jade lived on the other side of town. It would take her a while to get to the shop. Maybe I'll think of something, Megan told herself anxiously, putting on a CD. Something to make my best friend forgive me for thinking the unthinkable about her.

The shirt she had just ironed slid to the floor.

Megan was bending to pick it up when a pair of feet in blue shoes appeared in front of her eyes. Her head shot up.

Beth was standing over her, her face pale and strained, her eyes wide. She was wearing a long, black raincoat, and Megan could see that her hands were trembling.

Megan stood up. "How did you get in here?"

"A key," Beth whispered, standing perfectly still. "She has a key."

"Hello, Megan," Zoe Buffet said then, moving out of the shadowed staircase to stand beside Beth, smiling. "What are you up to, all alone in this hot little room? Ironing your prom dress?" Still smiling, she shook her head. "Not necessary, Megan. You won't be going."

Megan stared at Beth. "Beth?"

Beth burst into tears. There was an ugly bruise on her forehead from the accident. "She made me come, Megan! She got rid of the police officer, I don't know how, made me put this raincoat on over my hospital gown, and dragged me over here. She's . . . she's *crazy*, Megan! She killed Leah and attacked you and Lily and now. . ."

"Shut up!" Zoe said coldly.

"I don't get it. . ." Megan began, but in the next second, Zoe had her arm in a tight grip, Beth's arm in another grip, and was dragging both of them to the long, narrow, open window leading to the fire escape.

"Beth is going to push you, Megan," Zoe said matter-of-factly, "and then she's going to jump, because she is overwhelmed with guilt." She shook her head again, mournfully this time. "Such a tragedy. So sad, too bad, but . . . can't be helped."

Megan was strong and, except for her stiff knee, healthy. But Zoe, just as Adrienne had said, had the strength of madness and her fingers held on like giant pliers. She pushed both girls through the window at the same time, and then joined them on the fire escape, never letting go for an instant.

Below them, a car door slammed, then another. Two people got out of one car, a lone driver from the second car. The driver called out to the pair. Megan recognized the voice.

It was Dan's. Her knees caved with relief. Adrienne must have told him to pick her up here. Thank God!

She would have called out to him then, if Zoe hadn't sucked in her breath, muttered, "Damn!" and said through her teeth, "Make one sound and you die this very second, do you understand?"

Megan clamped her lips together. But at least he was down there. She felt a little less alone. Even if he did happen to look up, would he be able to see what was going on?

"Hey, Brandon," Dan called, "I didn't know you were back in town."

Brandon? Zoe's brother! Right down there in the courtyard, unaware that above him stood his sister, preparing to kill two people. "I got back last night. I took my last exam on Wednesday. Great to have that over with. So, what are you doing out here in the dark?"

Their voices lowered, and Megan had to strain to hear. But she picked up bits and pieces. The boy with Brandon was from his school, someone named "Jack".

Megan heard Dan say, "So, you're here in Glenview to take Zoe to the prom, right?"

Brandon's friend laughed. "Me? Are you kidding? I'm here to visit a girl I met through Brandon, and trust me, it's not his sister. I was her prom date last year. Never again! And believe me, no one else from our school will be taking her,

224

either. I spread the word. That girl is a loose cannon. Something seriously out of whack there, take my word for it."

Zoe's own brother agreed. "It's not her fault though. She's always had every single thing she ever wanted. Never learned how to deal with life not going exactly the way she wants it to. She has no concept of that at all."

Dan said to Brandon, "I guess I got it wrong. I thought she was going with Jack. She asked me, just a few days ago." He uttered a short laugh. "At a funeral, actually. I thought that was pretty weird. I had to tell her no, I was going with someone else. When I talked to her the next day, she said she was going with a friend of her brother's. I thought she said his name was Jack."

Megan turned to stare at Zoe. Zoe had asked Dan? At the funeral?

She remembered, then, the look of stupefied shock on Zoe's face at the cemetery. That hadn't been because of Leah. It was because she couldn't believe that Dan had refused to be her prom date.

Zoe's mouth was grim, her eyes narrowed. She stared back at Megan as if daring her to say what she was thinking.

Megan took the dare. Looking Zoe full in the face, she said slowly, her words tinged with awe, "You don't have a date for the prom, do you?"

Twenty-Seven

Zoe didn't answer Megan.

But below them, Brandon said, "The thing is, I can't keep up with who Zoe's prom date is. First she told me she was going with you, Dan. Then she called me later to say she wasn't, that Michael Danz was taking her. That was before I heard about what happened to Leah. The next time she called, she said she'd changed her mind again and was going with David Goumas."

On the fire escape, Megan's body was seized with a violent tremor. If Zoe hadn't been standing so close their arms bumped, she would have screamed.

"Then," Brandon continued, "my mum called and she said that Zoe's date for the prom was someone named Jordan Nelson. I don't know him. Zoe never mentioned him to me. So don't ask me who she's going with because I can't tell the players without a scorecard. The thing is, Dan, the last I heard, she was going with *you*. Told me that herself. You're telling me that's not true? You're taking someone else?"

Megan held her breath.

"I am definitely taking someone else. I'm here to pick her up, as a matter of fact. She works over there." Megan saw Dan point towards the shop.

"1 locked the door and turned off the downstairs lights," Zoe whispered in her ear. "He can't get in. When he goes round to the front and Brandon goes into the restaurant, you two are history. In the meantime, back inside you girls go. I can't have them seeing you."

Zoe dragged them both over the window-sill. Beth tumbled to the floor. Megan staggered over to lean against the wall next to the ironing board, careful to keep it between her and Zoe. Stall, she told herself, stall! Dan won't give up when he finds the door locked. He won't!

But she wasn't that sure. Maybe he'd think they'd got their signals crossed and, after a while, would return to her house.

That couldn't happen. If it did, she and Beth were done for.

"You don't have a date?" Megan repeated, keeping her eyes on Zoe, dreading any sudden moves on Zoe's part.

Zoe reached down to lift a pair of scissors off one of the shelves, slowly, as if she were in no hurry. "Of course I do. You heard Brandon. I'm going with Dan."

"She's crazy!" Beth cried softly from where she lay on the floor below the window. "She killed Leah and attacked you and Lily and tried to frame me for it, all because she didn't have a date. No one *asked* her!" Beth's upper lip curled with scorn. "No one wanted to take her."

Zoe looked at her calmly. "That's not true. They *all* wanted to. But they all assumed I'd already been asked. Because I've *always* gone to the prom. Every prom since I was a freshman. Three seniors asked me when I was only in ninth grade," she added proudly.

"Yeah, but not this time," Beth said harshly. "When you realized what was happening, you freaked out. And killed Leah so you could go with Michael."

"That is *not* what happened." Zoe's voice remained calm. "She just fell, that's all. And what *you* don't know, Miss Smartypants, is that I thought I *was* going. Until it was too late. Almost too late. I thought Michael was taking me."

Beth's eyes widened. "Michael? Michael Danz? But he. . ." Enlightenment dawned. "You? That was *you*, stabbing Leah in the back with Michael?" She sat up, accusing eyes on Zoe. "But you were her best friend!"

Zoe waved the scissors idly back and forth. "Best . . . west . . . nest . . . test . . . crest . . ." she murmured lazily.

Beth and Megan exchanged anxious glances.

". . . pest!" Zoe finished triumphantly. "I thought it was

only fair that Michael keep his word to me. But Leah refused to let him take me. Then she fell." Her eyes took on a dreamy look, and she continued to wave the scissors back and forth in front of her. "It wouldn't have been right for me to help her when she'd refused to help me by doing what was right. Michael *promised* me." She looked at Megan with innocent eyes. "Shouldn't Leah have seen to it that he kept his word?"

"Yes," Megan said sympathetically, "he should have, Zoe." Then, "Why did you leave a Quartet badge on the deck and under Lily's arm? What was that for? You didn't leave one at the bin."

"Well, of course not, Megan. *You* were never a part of our little group. Just Leah and Lily, Beth and I. We were our own solid little quartet. At least," Zoe added bitterly, "I *thought* we were. I left the badges there to remind them of a pact we made once, a long time ago. Leaving one at the bin would have been silly, because you weren't one of us."

When neither girl said anything, Zoe went on without emotion, "I never meant to hurt Leah, really. She was ignoring Michael, so busy with all her activities, and he came to me one night to cry on my shoulder. One thing led to another and, well, no one else had asked me to the prom because they all thought I'd already been invited and Michael said he would break his date with Leah and take me, so I kept seeing him. "But," her voice hardened, "he didn't *do* it. He didn't tell her. So I had to." She stopped waving the scissors. "She didn't take it very well."

"Dan isn't taking you, either," Beth said harshly. "He's taking Megan. He never wanted to take you, or he would have asked."

"That's not true!" Zoe shouted, her face changing, twisting with rage, her eyes wide. "I *am* going with Dan! He's waiting for me right now, at my house. I promised him I'd bring my dress and show it to him. Only. . ." She looked confused. ". . .only I don't know where it is. I stole it to put it in your boot with the others, and I don't know what happened to it after the accident." She laughed maniacally. "That was a stroke of luck for me, wasn't it? That silly accident, with the boot popping open! I saw the whole thing. I was following Beth, so I could watch when the police searched her boot. I was parked right up the street when Jade whipped round that corner and slammed into Beth's car." Remembering, her eyes glittered. "I laughed so much. . ."

"Zoe," Megan said evenly, "if Dan is waiting for you, you should probably hurry. I brought your dress back here after the accident. I knew you'd be needing it. It's hanging right downstairs, beside the cash register. Go ahead. Take your dress and go and meet Dan."

For the first time, Zoe looked uncertain. "Yes, I should do that," she said slowly, and turned to replace the scissors on the shelf.

"Meg?" Dan's voice, shouting. "Are you in there? The door's locked. Let me in, OK?"

Zoe gripped the scissors more tightly. The uncertainty gone, she whirled to face Megan. "Now I remember why I came here!" she hissed. "To get rid of *you*! If I don't, you could trick Dan again, like you did before. Trick him into taking you to the prom when he really wants to go with me." Holding the scissors up, she began walking towards Megan. "I can't let that happen. You can understand that, can't you?"

"No, Zoe," Megan said wearily, tiring of the cat-and-mouse game. "Frankly, I can't. It is just a dance. That's all it is."

"Oh, no," Zoe said softly, "that's not true. It's much, much more than that. And as for my friends," she added bitterly, "they were going to go without me. All of them. We'd always done everything together. We'd gone to every prom together. I couldn't believe they were going to break our solemn pact by going while I sat at home alone."

"Zoe, that's crazy!" Beth cried. "None of us *knew* you weren't going! You lied the whole time. You even bought a dress when we did. We thought you were going with a friend of Brandon's. And look who's talking about breaking a pact. Were you or were you not seeing Michael behind Leah's back?"

"That wasn't my fault. It was hers. And I didn't tell you I didn't have a date because then everyone in school would have known. They would have laughed at me."

Beth sagged against the wall, wiping a hand across her eyes as if she suddenly couldn't see. "We wouldn't have laughed at you. We would have made sure you had a date."

"I don't need *charity!*" Zoe shrieked, her eyes dark with rage. "Haven't I just *proved* to you that I can get my own date? *Haven't* I?"

"You got the insecticide from Beth's garage?" Megan asked, edging closer to the ironing board. It still stood between her and Zoe.

"You have to go out onto the fire escape," Zoe said unemotionally, leaving Megan's question unanswered. "Both of you. Now! With the two of you out of the way, I'll be queen for sure."

Megan stared at her. "Zoe, you can't be queen. You already have been. The rule at Glenview is, no one has that honour twice."

Zoe stared right back at her, her expression blank. "Well, *that's* just not true, Megan. I have never, ever been prom queen. You must have me mixed up with someone else.

232

That's one of the reasons I have to be sure to be there this time. This is my last chance to be queen."

Zoe's picture had been in the paper when she was selected prom queen. Megan remembered it very well. Zoe had looked really beautiful.

"No, Zoe," she said forcefully. "You have already been queen. You've just forgotten." A risky move on her part, she knew. Would pushing Zoe this way snap her back to reality? Or would it just make her angrier?

It made her angrier.

Megan's heart sank as Zoe's face reddened, and her eyes narrowed into tiny little slits of hatred. "That can't be true! You're lying, you have to be lying! You just don't want me to go with Dan, like Leah wouldn't let me go with Michael!"

And then, scissors held up, she rushed at Megan.

The ironing board shook as Zoe strained against it, reaching for Megan, the shiny blades poised above Megan's head.

Megan recoiled, forcing her body back against the wall as close as she could get. But she realized instantly what a mistake that was, and instead lunged forward. As she did so, she kicked out with one leg, crying out in pain as her stitches pulled, and slammed her foot against the ironing board's criss-crossed, wooden legs.

They gave way, folding instantly with a groan.

The scissors were no more than a centimetre from Megan's chest when the board collapsed. The blades raked a trail of red down Megan's left forearm as the ironing board and Zoe and the scissors crashed to the floor.

Someone was pounding on the door downstairs.

Ignoring the blood spilling from the gashes in her arm, Megan scooped up the iron that had fallen with the board and quickly, before a stunned Zoe could clear her head, yanked the girl's arms behind her back and wound the iron's cord around her wrists.

Then she ran downstairs to open the door.

Jade, stiff with hurt and anger, was standing there.

Dan, worry in his eyes, was right behind her.

"You are *not* going to believe this," Megan gasped, and let them in.

Twenty-Eight

Adrienne had outdone herself. When Megan saw her reflection in the full-length mirror on her mother's wardrobe door, she couldn't believe her eyes. The vivid blue dress had, of course, done its part, performing exactly as Megan had anticipated. But the hair helped, too, its limpness gone, falling to her shoulders in shiny, softly curled perfection. And the face . . . was that *her* face? Adrienne's light but expert touch had emphasized her best feature, her eyes, but enhanced her other features with her special magic. Megan knew she looked . . . well, actually, she looked pretty. Really pretty.

And even if she hadn't known that then, it would have hit home the minute she saw the expression on Dan's face when she came down the stairs and he looked up at her and sounded a soft "Wow".

Dinner at Impeccable Tastes was wonderful, except for a

brief moment when they got out of the car and found themselves facing the bin. But Dan had taken her arm and hurried her away from there and then everything was all right again.

And now, here she was, moving across the gym floor in Dan's arms, smiling, laughing, talking, just like everyone else at the prom. The tables were beautiful, decorated with floor-length cloths and the tiny miniature yearbooks. Framed posters of films known only for their happy endings were hung on the walls throughout the gym. Bouquets of blue and yellow flowers donated by Quartet's silent partners from their own gardens joined the tiny yearbooks on each table. Generous of them, Megan thought, since not one of their daughters was at the dance. Even Beth, completely cleared of any wrongdoing, had opted not to come.

"She said she'd feel funny," Dan had told Megan when she asked about Beth, "since none of her friends would be here."

Megan had asked him, long after the police had taken Zoe away and everything had been explained and Jade had been apologized to until Megan was blue in the face, why he had never told her that Zoe had invited him to the dance.

"I didn't think it was important," he had said.

Unfortunately, Zoe had.

Jade danced by in Joseph's arms. He was beaming. Megan had told Jade about the phone call, pointing out that Joseph must really care or he wouldn't have embarrassed himself that way. She didn't take the turquoise dress from the cupboard where Adrienne had hidden it until after Jade announced that she had asked and Joseph had accepted.

OK, so the night wouldn't be the dance of Jade's dreams. But she looked as if she was having a good time. Adrienne had done her hair and make-up, too, and she looked lovely.

A girl named Elizabeth Connor, who Megan knew only slightly, was chosen as queen. The crown seemed to suit her. She stood up on the stage, smiling, her date beside her, and for one small moment Megan pictured Beth's drawing and wished things had turned out differently for Beth.

Megan and Dan, hands clasped, were watching, smiling, as the king and queen began the next dance. They were about to walk out on the floor after the first few bars of music, when a stir in the room caught their attention. Megan was the first to turn round, her eyes scanning the candlelit gym for some sign of a disturbance. When her gaze moved to the doorway, she gasped and her grip on Dan's hand tightened abruptly. He turned round.

Zoe Buffet was standing in the doorway.

"Dan?" Megan asked, drawing closer to him.

"Out on bail," he said cryptically. "Her father got her out. She's not going to be charged with murder, just manslaughter, so while she's waiting for the psychiatric

237

evaluation, the judge let her go home. Her parents are supposed to be watching out for her. I didn't tell you because I didn't want to ruin your evening. Sorry. If I'd had any idea she'd show up here, I'd have warned you."

As more people turned to see what was happening, a hush fell over the huge gym. The music continued to play, but the king and queen stopped dancing, as did everyone else. In just seconds, all eyes were on the entrance to the gym.

Though Zoe's dress was black, it wasn't the pretty dress she had bought at Quartet. Because she didn't have that dress, Megan realized. She had left without it that horrible night, in the custody of the police. That dress was probably at the police station, in the evidence room.

The dress Zoe was wearing was full-length, long-sleeved and matronly, and at least two sizes too large. It hung on her like a sack, and one shoulder had slipped off, causing the dress to hang at an odd angle around her neck.

That's her mother's dress, Megan thought. Zoe is wearing one of her mother's dresses.

That was not the worst of it, she saw as Zoe, a vacant smile on her face, began moving into the room. Something was very wrong with her face. Gorgeous, impeccable Zoe had applied make-up with a heavy, disoriented hand. As she drew closer, Megan saw with horrified awe that her mouth was outlined to nearly twice its normal size with thick, red, greasy lipstick. Her eyebrows were heavily outlined in dark pencil, and thick blusher in an orangey shade had been applied to her entire cheek area on one side of her face, to only the cheekbone on the other side, giving her face as lopsided a look as the oversized dress gave her body.

Jade and Joseph had moved up to stand beside Megan and Dan. "Oh, no," Jade whispered as Zoe walked unsteadily but purposely towards the silent, staring crowd, "she's wearing a crown, Megan!"

Zoe had placed on the blonde hair that badly needed washing and hung lank and lacklustre around the garishly made-up face, a homemade "crown". It looked like the effort of a small child, cheap, gold foil covering what was probably cardboard cut into a crown shape, bent into a circle, and stapled.

"Oh, man," Joseph breathed.

One hand holding up the edge of the ugly black dress so that she wouldn't trip over it, Zoe moved daintily towards David Goumas and his date.

"Why, David, you rascal!" Zoe said, her voice low and sweet but audible since the band, aware now that something out of the ordinary was happening, had stopped playing. The room had grown as quiet as a library. "Whatever are you doing with this pretty little thing? I was so sure that, with darling Lily incapacitated, you would be calling me to be your date for the prom." She smiled up at him, and one hand moved forward to gently stroke his cheek. "I guess you must have thought I was already otherwise engaged, am I right, darling David? I forgive you, I really do."

The pair remained frozen as Zoe moved on to the next couple. One by one, the bizarrely made-up and costumed girl went from couple to couple, smiling, scolding the boys, dismissing the girls with a flick of her finger or a contemptuous smile, speaking only to their dates in soft, sweet tones.

When she came to Dan and Megan, Megan instinctively took a step backwards. But she didn't let go of Dan's hand.

"And you, my darling Dan," Zoe said sternly, shaking a finger in Dan's face, "I am having trouble dismissing your treachery. Why, everyone here," waving a hand to encompass the semicircle of onlookers, "knows that you and I were meant to attend these festivities together, isn't that right, everyone?" Her eyes behind thick coats of mascara flicked over the crowd and then returned to Dan's face. "But I don't blame you, sweetie." The smile disappeared and her face darkened. "I know who's behind such treachery. My so-called dearest friends, who swore they would never betray me and then did, anyway. I have taken care of the matter. Don't give it another thought. Now that I'm here, though," the smile returned as she gazed up at him with assurance, "you *are* going to dance with me, aren't you, Dan?" Holding the folds of her skirt out around her, she twirled flirtatiously before him. "I got all dressed up for you. Do you like it?"

"It's very nice," Dan said. "You look very nice, Zoe."

Zoe seemed then to become aware of Megan, standing at Dan's side. Her eyes narrowed. "Who are *you*? What are you doing with Dan? Go away!" She reached out and slapped at Megan's hand, still in Dan's. "Let go of him!"

"Zoe!" a voice from the doorway called. Heads turned. Megan recognized the couple striding quickly across the floor. A tall, authoritative-looking woman, expensively dressed in a linen suit, and an equally tall gentleman: Zoe's parents. Both faces were anxious, and, Megan thought, embarrassed. "Zoe, dear, what are you doing here? How did you sneak past us?"

Zoe turned. "Oh, hello, Mother. Father. I can't leave just yet. I haven't danced with Dan. You will just have to wait." She turned back to Dan, smiling up at him expectantly.

"No," her mother said firmly, "Zoe, we have to go now."

Dan looked down at Megan, a question in his eyes.

She nodded. "It's OK," she said softly. "Go ahead."

Then Megan stood aside as Dan led Zoe, in her bizarre garb, out onto the dance floor. He waved a hand towards the band and they began playing a slow melody. The coloured ball above the dancers' heads spun gently, surrounding them with a soft rainbow glow.

Zoe laid her head on Dan's chest as he spun her slowly around the floor. For those brief moments, at least, all the rage and the hatred seemed to have drained out of her, and she looked content.

Megan felt tears stinging her eyes and, when she looked at Jade, she was surprised to see tears there, too, sliding slowly down Jade's cheeks.

No one in the gym uttered a word. There was only the sweet, poignant music and the couple gliding along the floor, all eyes on them.

Zoe's parents, watching from the sidelines with pain in their faces, waited patiently.

When the music ended, Zoe's head lifted, she looked up at Dan and, smiling, said, "Thank you. That was very nice." Then she turned towards her parents and said, "I'm very tired now. I'd like to go home, please."

They took her home.

Epilogue

It might have been an hour, maybe less, before spirits lifted again and the fun resumed. But it did resume. It was prom night, their "happy ending" to four years of high school, and after a while the image of the sad, sick girl standing in the doorway in a dress too big for her, her face a clown mask, faded. Laughter and music and chatter replaced the painful silence.

Megan, dancing in Dan's arms, had no idea what would happen with them. Maybe they would go their separate ways when college began in the autumn. But as long as she lived, a part of her would always love him for what he had done for Zoe.

Zoe would spend the rest of her life paying for what she'd done. One little dance didn't seem like much to give her in comparison.

"So," Dan said, looking down at her with a smile, "you

243

never did answer me about softball. I need you on my team this summer. How about it?"

"Well, let's see," she answered slowly, "I have to work at Quartet, and get ready for college. But I might be able to squeeze in some time to play."

Jade danced by, smiling. Megan remembered what good sports Sophie and Lucy had been, finally, about not attending the prom. "There's just one condition," she added quickly. "Jade, Sophie, and Lucy play, too. We're a package deal." Because we're a quartet, too, she thought. Like Zoe and her friends. But I want us to *stay* that way, for as long as we possibly can. "Deal?"

"Are they any good?"

Megan grinned up at him. "The best. Like me, they are the very best."

"Done," he said, and laughed.

LOOK OUT FOR
MORE

HORROR HIGH

IF YOU DARE . . .

NO ONE HERE GETS OUT ALIVE

CAROLINE B COONEY

HORROR HIGH

TOXIC BEAUTY

NO ONE HERE GETS OUT AliVE

CAROLINE B COONEY

HORROR HIGH

KilleR insTincT

NO ONE HERE GETS OUT ALIVE

R.L. STINE

HORROR HIGH

GRAVE INTENTIONS

NO ONE HERE GETS OUT ALIVE

R.L. STINE

HORROR HIGH

FATAL KISS

NO ONE HERE GETS OUT ALIVE

R. L. STINE

HORROR HIGH

DEADLY RUMOURS